Battleground State

NATASHA PATEL

ISBN-13 978-1481234054
ISBN-10 1481234056
LCCN 2012923681

Cover design by Angie-O Creations at www.angieocreations.com
Author photo by Kelsey Edwards Photography at
www.kelseyedwardsphoto.com
Formatting by Jason G. Anderson at www.jasonga.com

To all the volunteers who labored alongside us and turned the campaign into a family reunion.

"All the great battlegrounds of the civil rights movement were in the South. In the North there seem to be a great many people with little faith, people who have almost given up, people who feel that they have little to hold on to or believe in. They never went through what we went through. They never tasted directly what we tasted. So they simply do not believe." John Lewis, 1996, *Walking with the Wind: A Memoir of the Movement*

CHAPTER 1

At the age of 30, Lily DeMarco moved from the corner of East 77th and 1st Avenue in Manhattan to her parents' basement in Paterson, New Jersey. This was the second time she had moved into the well-lit, partially subterranean section of her parents' home, which her parents euphemized as the "in-law suite" because of its mini kitchen and separate bedroom, or more vaguely, "the downstairs." The first time was at the age of 16 when her brother David had moved out of it as he left for college, and she had lived there until her own ascent to New York University. Her brother later returned after graduation from Colorado State. He stayed for two years before moving out to California, leaving behind his snowboard, which cluttered the hallway that led to the laundry room. Despite having resided in the basement for nearly two months, Lily still stumbled on the snowboard's footholds as she carried her laundry down the hall, reminding herself each time to list it for sale online. The basement not only served as a holding station for the DeMarco children but also a part-time yoga studio for her semi-retired father and, for her mother, a library of do-it-yourself magazines dating back at least fifteen years. There were seven summer editions dedicated to the best methods for cleaning the grease off the charcoal grill, as if each year some new discovery in the hot dog and hamburger grilling styles of Americans unearthed a new iron brush.

It wasn't as if Lily didn't have anywhere else to live. To the contrary, she owned five hundred and twenty five square feet in the island of Manhattan, but her layoff at Heels & Ellsworth LLP quickly brought an end to that former life. Now, after paying the mortgage, monthly maintenance, and the occasional assessment by the co-op board, she netted $175 a month from her current tenant, Kuang Wei Chiu, who had introduced himself as Jerry, a Taiwanese ingénue who, before teaching at the New York Technical Institute, invented a network box that allowed users to play their own music in place of the original movie soundtrack while watching a movie and still simultaneously chatting online with friends over the movie and the music. She was surprised at how quickly she had grown accustomed to life in the basement. She had evolved from the early days of sheer mortification when, during her denial stage, she applied to every job posted on the internet, from CEO of a fledgling internet foot spa delivery service to the hostess at 'Ahoy Mate seafood restaurant. She now had a room equipped with a television, her old bed, and an additional $415 a week from unemployment.

"The Lily of two months ago would never be content to surf the television all day," Gabe's voice guided via the speaker on her Blackberry, a departing gift by her ex-employer.

"I surf the internet all day long, too." She glanced at the five open windows flickering on her laptop. Her forehead began to ache. It was almost noon, and she hadn't emerged from her bedroom yet.

"Day 2 in that shirt?"

"Day 3." For the last three days, Lily had worn her old EJ's t-shirt and boxer shorts. She last wore this t-shirt on her brunch shift over three years ago. She was happy it still fit, albeit snugly.

"At least change into your Nacho Mama t-shirt. Their food was much better."

"Shouldn't you be tilling the land?" Gabe had more leisure time to chat on the phone since he was no longer employed by Buffalo Steers. He recently moved to Pennsylvania to help his uncle, a former executive at Goldbank who used his own buyout package to purchase 26 acres and convert the former landfill into an organic farm.

"Already done."

"Well, aren't you the productive one today."

"And aren't you the grumpy one."

"Sorry, I don't mean to be snappish, but may I remind you that I was fired?" The realization still steeped freshly in her waking mind. On occasion she would awake with the renewed feeling she had during her stay on holiday breaks from college, momentarily forgetting the reason she was living in parents' basement again. And then, just as she began to change out of her t-shirt, she would remember that this wasn't a break. She didn't have anything to which to return.

"You were laid off."

"Isn't that the same?"

"No. Fired is because of something you did. Laid off is because of something the company did, or didn't do, I guess. I was laid off too."

"That's different. Your company went bankrupt. Heels and Ellsworth is still operational on the 44th floor of the Met-Life building." She'd never been fired from anything before. She was re-elected to her high school's student council all four years on the promise of a soda machine in the band practice room.

"Tell people you're laid off. It's less of a ... hmm what's the word I'm looking for?"

"Taboo," she answered. "But it is the same to me. I wouldn't hire someone who had just been fired or laid off. Or whatever you call being let go involuntarily." Two months had passed since Mr. Davies had called her into his office and had asked her to sign the severance agreement. She had billed more hours than any other associate at the firm for the last three years. She had even skipped friends' weddings over a holiday weekend and relinquished her prized tickets to the Subway World Series, which pitted the Mets against the Yankees. When in the last six months she had suddenly stopped receiving Friday 5 p.m. phone calls to work over the weekend, she had knocked on every Partner's door announcing willingness to work on any kind of matter at any hour and in any form, toadying herself up like leftover turkey the week after Thanksgiving. Nothing. The Partners kept it for themselves. They circled any new client like vultures, devouring the few scraps of work that was offered.

"Do you miss your old life?" she asked. She missed their time together in New York. Every Monday at 6 p.m., they would meet at O'Reilly's on Lexington and 30th, exactly mid-point between their two offices, for a smoky Guinness and Guinness-battered fried fish, the one day a week she allowed herself fried food. They would scour the weekly event calendar and plan the shows they would want to see or the new restaurants they wanted to sample. They would recap any first or second dates they had over the weekend and advise each other on which guy seemed worthy of a next date, though most rarely made it past the third date. She had had only one significant relationship in her life, which ended when she graduated from college. It was Gabe who had advised her on her most important decisions in life so far — the slickest bicycle, the most fashionable prom dress, and the most profitable mutual funds in her 401k.

"I haven't tasted a Porterhouse or '83 Bordeaux in months. But I knew it was time to merge with the land, even if that means scooping toxic dump to make way for arugula."

"I'll just live out the rest of my life in Bergen County, New Jersey watching the five seasons of Ex-Housewives of the Jersey Shore."

"It is addictive. They cycle through courting, marriage, and divorce quicker than I can rotate my carrots. But, Lily, really, you just need get out of the house. Volunteer for something. You have a severance that will last you a little while."

"You sound like my mother."

"Tell Rita I'll be over in couple of weeks to examine the fabrics for the reupholster. And let Rick know that I have a Snow White tomato seedling plant for his garden. "

"Is it poisonous?"

"Not that I know of."

"Gabe, I earned a graduate degree and have four years of professional work experience. That's not counting the years I scooped ice cream in high school."

"It's a new world and-"

"Oh, and I interned for Representative Weissman. Too bad she's still not in office. I think she now works for Argon Pharm. Maybe they're hiring."

"It is an election year. You could make some phone calls."

She groaned. It was hard to forget that it was an election year. It was only May and her parents received several fundraising calls a day from the Democrats — the Congressional campaign, the Senate campaign, the national party, the state party, the county party, the individual Gubernatorial candidate, and the Democratic Presidential Nominee, Ramal Cady, probably the most charismatic candidate the Democrats had had in a generation.

Cady was someone who could levitate people with his oration, and offered the Democrats their best chance of winning in nearly a decade, since Roy Stafford's last term in office. At each rally, the host would warm-up the crowd by shouting "Are you crazy?" and the crowd would repeat, "We are crazy." "Are you ready?" "We are ready!" "We are crazy, ready for Cady!" It didn't take much. Cady represented the amalgamation of all of America's ideals — he was *the melting pot* of America. Born to a black schoolteacher mother and a Scottish military officer father, he was someone who could espouse Keynesian economics while drinking a Miller Beer. He spoke French and Korean *and* Spanish. He was born in Colorado, but was raised in Korea and France. He had studied economics at Stanford on a swimming scholarship, and then upon graduation returned to a Colorado ranch to wrangle cattle. After his graduation from Yale law school, he moved to

Detroit's south side and represented the community in an environmental class action case against the utility company, yielding the largest settlement in Michigan's history. There he met his wife, a lovely woman who also matched his intellect and experience, and to whom he remained uncompromisingly faithful. No opposition research had revealed a message, a photo, a tweet, or an email that hinted at even flirtation. Together they returned to Denver, where he served in the State House, then State Senate, then as Lieutenant Governor, where he cast the tie-breaking vote on the bill that instituted the first ever background checks and seven-day waiting period for a gun purchaser in the state. In spite of this, he was elected Governor and balanced the state's budget *and* still managed to achieve the highest college acceptance rate of Colorado high school graduates in state history. They had two pre-teen boys who spent their afternoons on the basketball court *and* served as youth church mentors. They recently adopted a three-year old girl from Malawi whose smile charmed even the most hardened city dweller. It was rumored that Cady's great-grandfather had been an Arapahoe Indian. Gaia could not have created a more perfect candidate for the Democratic establishment. Cady made Mother Teresa *and* Bill Gates appear inadequate. And while his career continued on an upward trajectory, Lily had been too consumed by her own professional demise to think anything more about him, other than that she would vote for him in November.

"Lily, the firm didn't work out. What do you want to do now?"

"I don't know." She thought she had wanted a successful career at a law firm, a comfortable lifestyle in New York, and eventually someone to share it all with. But now, her future was a blank slate.

"Just try something. Anything."

"I did see an internet posting by the local Democrats for volunteers. Maybe I'll swing by there on my way to the mall."

"Another lunch at Chick N' Bik?"

"Whatever they put in that cheese sauce is addictive."

"You used to only go there when you worked an overnighter. Now you're there every day."

"Gabe, I'm mourning."

"No, you're self-loathing. It's unattractive."

She knew he was right. But she didn't know how to snap out of it. "Maybe this is who I'm supposed to be. I don't know how this all happened." She glanced at her suit, which had been bought from a luxury department store for her interview with the firm, and was now sealed in dry-cleaning plastic, ready to be stored away in the back of her parents' basement bedroom closet. She remembered it had itched throughout the interview, as the Partner discussed the firm's unsurpassed growth in mortgage-backed securities driven by their major client Buffalo Steers, which in retrospect clearly portended her current predicament. She had majored in political science and economics, the perfect combination for law school. Or at least that was what her undergraduate career counselor had advised. She had aced the LSAT, which earned her admissions into a top-rated law school. She, her parents, and the federal government had spent a combined total of $225,000 on her education. She had been the obedient DeMarco child, who never stayed out past curfew and spent most Friday nights at the movies with her parents. She had only smoked pot once and coughed the entire time. What more could she do to ensure job security and stability?

"Lily, I just spent the morning churning ten drums of compost. I never thought the rancid smell of old lemon peels and coffee grounds mixed with cow manure could leave me wanting more, but I'm looking forward to the next ten this afternoon. Go by the office and let me know how it goes."

She admired his ability to adapt to any situation. While all the other employees were sneaking staplers, file folders, and flash drives into their briefcases and handbags, Gabe volunteered to assist in the liquidation of Buffalo Steers assets. He had always longed to be on stage before a microphone, and since his high school dream of being the next Barry Manilow didn't pan out, being an auctioneer for a day was the next best thing.

She surveyed her pre-college bedroom. Her mother had installed a few additional shelves to house David's soccer trophies. Her diplomas from both NYU undergrad and law school were framed and hung next to an old recruiting poster NYU had sent years ago. It quoted the old Bob Dylan song: *The times they are a-changin. Come change with us.* She pulled the poster from the wall, rolled it into the tiniest possible ball, and tossed it into the trash. She showered and changed into a crisp white collared shirt and khaki skirt, pulled her curly black hair into a hair band, grabbed her bag, and ascended to the main floor of the house.

Her parents' chatter subsided as she entered the kitchen. They smiled at her change of clothes. Her mother handed her a magazine. "Lily, what do you think of these sunlight panels? I'm thinking of installing one in the kitchen."

"Great idea, mom." She learned long ago to support her mother's renovation inclinations. If it was a bad idea, and she or her father said so, her mother would surely do it, like the time she installed a five-gallon food incinerator, which doubled as a compost, next to the refrigerator. It would eventually dawn on her mom that destroying the roof above their kitchen to make way for a sunlight may not be the best idea. But regardless, she admired her mother's efforts. Rita failed at more projects than she succeeded, and Lily wondered if the resilient gene had passed only to David.

"Let me help you," Lily said, and joined her mother's furious search for a measuring tape. After a few minutes of stumbling through the drawers and cabinets they found it. Rita left to find a ladder.

"Green tea?" Rick lifted the teakettle to pour her a cup.

"Still on coffee, Dad." She poured herself a cup and sat down with him at the breakfast nook. Two years ago, her father cut out meat, coffee, and even alcohol. Not that he ever ate one morsel or drank one sip more than the recommended daily allowance. But he was following guidelines for a longer life proclaimed by Jim Pharoah, MD, a TV doctor who singlehandedly saved the green tea industry from extinction.

Rita returned with the ladder and climbed to the second step.

"Need some help mom?"

"No, I've got it."

She had recently helped her mother paint the kitchen a lively pale yellow, and the fresh paint smell had finally subsided. She now smelled the rosemary and parsley that had been planted in the window box. She watched the herbs dance under the wind from the open window. Rita didn't need a sunlight; the kitchen was already bright and full of life.

Unlike the kitchen at Heels & Ellsworth, which had been stripped of its stainless steel European appliances and replaced with old domestic plastic ones, bought second-hand. The refrigerator had been filled with individually labeled milk cartons, as the firm no longer provided such amenities. The coffee, still free, had maintained a constant burnt smell. The walls were left bare, just spotted with empty hooks, a reminder of the original contemporary art they used to hold. Only a couple of round tables had remained. The Partners had removed the couches to avoid the naps by unoccupied associates.

She recalled having found Bea, the secretary she shared with Mr. Davies, sitting quietly at the table, her cup trembling as she sipped her coffee.

"I haven't made photocopies in a week," she had confessed. "I haven't filed anything in over a month. I just sit at my desk and stare at the computer screen for seven hours, with a break for lunch. Then before I leave, I pop my head into Mr. Davies' office and ask if there is anything else he needs, and he says *No*." She was the best secretary the firm had, and until that moment, Lily had thought she was safe. "I don't play Solitaire. I don't shop on-line. I just sit there."

She had been a better person than Lily. Lily had spent much of her last month's paycheck on the new discounted fashion website, Pizzazz. "You work for the Chairman of the firm and you've been here for 22 years. You're safe," she had assured.

"Rosalie starts college in the fall," she had said.

On Lily's last day, when Mr. Davies had asked her to sign the severance agreement, she had willingly obliged. She said nothing while Mr. Davies gave his speech about the economy and the finances of the firm. She nodded in appreciation when he offered to give her a recommendation for the next job. She replied with thanks when he said good luck in her career, incapable of clever words of indignation or a dramatic exit. He then asked to see Bea, who smiled with composure and glided into the office with ease. Lily slumped down in the reception area unable to leave. She stared at a painting of a bare tree against a black grey sky. A ray of light shined on the three remaining brown leaves that clung to the tree branch. She wiped away the tear that had trickled down her face. She'd never cried in the office before. Not when Mr. Davies had chastised her for a typo or when the client had replaced her with another associate with whom he had played golf. She had missed the warning signs at Heels and Ellsworth, buried in her own security of confidence and credentials. Bea came out of the office with the severance agreement in hand and sat beside her on the couch. She cradled Lily's shoulders. "I've always liked that painting," she had said. "I bet those leaves have a soft landing."

Lily hoped Bea had found another job.

"Lil, want to go for a bike ride?" Rick asked. He laid a road map on the table, which he had marked, to scale, for water fountains, public restrooms, and scenic overlooks. "If we take Route 9 to Palisades and then cross over to Route 17, we can be sure to see that rock formation with the eagle carvings. By the Oneida tribe, I believe." Rick never stumbled onto anything. She had always been his trusty assistant helping him to plan their family's bike rides, camping trips, and beach vacations meticulously. David would groan at the stifling structure and Rita would discover inspirations for new projects. At this moment, however, she wanted to rip his map into two and tell him just to ride.

"I'm going to stop by the Democratic Headquarters here. See if I can do anything."

"That's wonderful, dear! They'll be so lucky to have you," said Rita. "Make sure you tell them you worked for Representative Weissman."

"It was just an internship."

"And you graduated with honors in Political Science," her mother continued.

"I'm just going to volunteer. It's not an actual job."

"Lily, I think it's great you're finally getting out of the house. Remember, you don't have to jump right into the next thing. You can live in the downstairs as long as you need," said Rick.

"Dad, I've haven't jumped into anything anywhere. I've planned every step of my life and look where that got me. I'm 30 years old living in my parents' basement."

"It's an in-law suite, dear," said Rita.

"Lily, it's not your fault or anyone else's why you're here," said Rick.

"Yes it is. If it's not mine, then it's that guidance counselor at NYU, or Mr. Davies who mismanaged H&E until five associates were left standing."

"Things are just bad right now. They'll turn around. They always do."

How could she convince her dad that the ground under all of them had shifted and she was still trying to regain her balance? David had been the wiser one. Bucking any expectation by her parents, as well as society, to live out of a suitcase and his station wagon, shuttling his saxophone from one city to the next, bartending along the way.

"Ok to take the car?" She shared her dad's Toyota, as Rita's van was currently packed with a weed trimmer, six 2 x 4s, a sewing machine, and a wooden trunk.

Her father nodded. "Take this lavender I pulled from the garden. It'll help you relax."

Dried herbs could not save her future. But she took the neatly bundled package. The strong sweet smell jolted her to action. "I'll report back later."

She rolled down the window and fiddled with the radio tuner until finding NPR. *The latest economic indicators suggest …* that the economy sucks. Mr. Davies had been wrong when she first met him three years ago. Mortgage backed securities had disappeared right from under those who created them. No other law firm was hiring. No company was hiring. The only reason she billed 2800 hours a year preparing those loan and finance documents is because that's what they had asked of her. She owed it to the firm who paid her handsomely enough to repay her student loans and provide for a comfortable life in New York. Didn't she? Isn't that why she went to law school? She no longer remembered. In the time it had taken merely to schedule an interview with public interest organizations, the law firms had courted her with expensive French bistro dinners and rare blends of red wine. They had pursued her like a dog in heat needing her brain and eagerness to generate revenue. At the time, Heels and Ellsworth was actually the easiest job to obtain. She had had more difficulty securing the Sunday brunch shift at E.J.'s Luncheonette.

She arrived in the parking lot of the Democratic Headquarters, a quaint old building which previously had been a fishing supply store, but was now rented out to the Bergen County Democratic Party. It was tucked between a hair salon, which was already teeming with ladies, and an Italian deli, whose cumin scented meatballs wafted through its doors. Patriotic banners hung from the eaves of the old fish store. The door was propped open, waiting for her to come inside, but she remained in the car. All her former colleagues had taken their severance in bliss. Christine opened a Greek pastry stand at the farmer's market. James started a Philippine martial arts studio. David wrote a tour guide to historical baseball fields. All were classmates from law school and who had jumped at the early severance package to follow a hunch or a dream. They had hatched their plans during their daily 3 p.m.

coffee breaks at the cafe down the street, away from the ears and eyes of the Partners. She had listened attentively as the three of them excitedly planned their Plan B lives, unable to imagine her own. And now they were all proudly living them from their studio apartments in Queens. She envied their ability to take such leaps. The only leap she'd taken in her adult life so far was crossing over the Hudson River from Paterson, New Jersey to the East Village, then to the Upper East Side, back over the Hudson to Paterson. By the age of 30 she had arrived full circle in her life, one that only took an hour to drive. Until now, she hadn't thought she needed a Plan B. She grabbed her bag and got out of the car.

"Lily! Lily DeMarco? Is that you?" Even after 12 years, she could recognize that eager, friendly voice anywhere. She heard it cheering at the school's pep rallies, or laughing with friends against the lockers, or explaining calculus to the student in the next seat, and she could never forget when it persuaded her to serve as the Vice-President of the Student Council. Only one person could be President, and that was Naomi Ellis.

"Hi, Naomi." She was roped by a toddler, a miniature Naomi, who was unwilling to let go of her leg. Both Naomi and toddler had golden auburn hair, well-defined features, and an anatomy that was affixed in perfect proportion.

"What are you doing back here?" She hugged Lily firmly, but warmly.

"Well, I'm, visiting my parents and well, visiting…"

"We must get lunch then. I'd love to catch up and hear how you're doing! I hear you're a lawyer now. Wow. Are you married? Any children? "

"No."

"Well, of course not, you're living large in New York! Who wants to have children when you've got New York. I always wished I had moved to the city for even just a couple of years. But I met Andy in college and, well, this little Eva is our second." She patted Eva's head like a puppy at Christmas. Eva grinned. "Jake is with his father at soccer."

"That's great.

"How long will you be in town for? Let me see my schedule." She pulled out her Blackberry to check her calendar.

"Well, I'm not sure. I'm helping my mom build this skylight and things are really busy."

"Oh, Rita is so wonderful with her projects. I still remember our Student Council float for the Homecoming parade. An entire replica of the House of Representatives."

"Right."

"Why don't you come over for Sunday brunch? We live on the North side, by the lake. We could go for a walk around the bank, or even take the boat out. Andy would love to meet you."

"I'm not sure I have the time." Lily took out her own Blackberry.

"It won't be as glamorous as those New York brunches, but I do make a tasty western omelet, with coriander."

"No, that does sound wonderful." What would she chat about over spicy eggs and a boat ride? She was unemployed and living in her parents' basement, while Jerry hosted dim sum parties for New York Technical faculty members in her apartment.

"I just can't because I have to get back to the city early on Sunday. Work."

"Of course. I understand. That is one thing I don't envy about you New Yorkers. How much you have to work. But it so great to see you, Lily, really. Law school and an amazing job in New York. Sometimes, I wonder if Andy and I ever broke up, what I would do. I haven't worked in 5 years." Suddenly, Naomi's face darkened to a reddish cast. She was genuinely concerned.

"Naomi, you'd be fine." Lily realized that the girl who got everything she wanted in in high school got everything she wanted afterwards too. The movies lied.

"Thanks Lily. Well let me get little Eva off to her appointment. Next time you're in town, we must plan something."

"We will." When she had a job or had done something worth discussing.

She walked into the county party headquarters determined to bring democracy to Bergen County. The sounds of sharp, quick, voices seeking contributions emanated through the air. Large wooden tables, the kind she sat at in art class in high school, were arranged in line with church pew precision. Men and women were dressed identically in long shorts, collared cotton button downs, and sport sandals with socks. They held the telephone receivers close to their mouths, speaking louder than necessary. She hadn't seen this many land lines in one room since the Jerry Lewis telethon. No one was under the age of 50.

"Can I help you, dear?" asked a lady who was tallying up the fundraising sheets.

"Yes, I'm here to volunteer. Do you need any?"

"Dear, we always need volunteers!" Lily scanned the room. Where were all the interns? The Cady supporters? You couldn't escape their pledge requests on the streets of New York.

"What would you like me to do?"

"How about selling our t-shirts and gold pins?" The lady gathered the t-shirts, still in boxes, and the pins, still in plastic wrapping, and dragged them to a small card table near the front door. "We've been so busy, I haven't had to the time to do it myself."

They arranged the t-shirts with department store precision and displayed the gold pins in its own plastic jewelry case and a display mirror.

"Here's the cash box."

"Do you have a calculator?" Lily asked.

The lady looked at her skeptically. "Here's a pad and paper for calculations. And here's our sign. I designed it myself." She proudly affixed a poster of a donkey, with BCDP printed on its behind, kicking with its hind legs an elephant's trunk, printed with BCRP.

Lily settled into her chair and task. For the next two hours, only three people walked through the door. The delivery guy from the Italian deli distributed meatball hoagies and peppermints to everyone. He paused to examine the gold pin, holding it up to his earlobe for sizing, but when she explained it was only a pin, he set it back down. A four year old, with pink ice trickling down his shirt, ran through the doors begging to sit in his grandfather's lap while he fundraised for democracy in Paterson, New Jersey. His grandfather did purchase a child's BCDP t-shirt as a memento. And the husband of the lady who designed the t-shirt had an urgent need to borrow her SUV in exchange for his sedan. He had no time to browse Lily's offerings. Lily refolded the t-shirts and polished the gold pins. Then she gathered the details on famed teenage rock star Brady Smith's rehab and subsequent child visitation schedule from all three sources – Celebrity Week, Update!, and The A-Squad. She returned to the lady sitting at her tally desk.

"Is there something else you would like me to do? It's not particularly busy over there."

"Well, dear, all the telephone chairs are taken."

"Oh."

"You know. You may want to talk with the Cady campaign office."

"I didn't know they had an office in New Jersey."

"They don't. Their office is in New York. Harlem, I think. But I do hear they are actually hiring people."

"Really?" Even though it was only a 30-minute drive to the George Washington Bridge, she hadn't set foot in Manhattan since the day she turned over her keys to Jerry. It was almost 3 p.m. She would miss the season 2 marathon of Ex-Housewives of Jersey Shore. But she did have a copy of her resume in her bag. Maybe she just needed to think about it a little longer, while watching season 2. She thanked the lady and sat back inside the car. Yet, as her mind remained indecisive, her car was soon making its way over the bridge.

Once inside Manhattan, she drove in the opposite direction of Harlem, traveling South toward the tip of the island. A stop at Chick N' Bik would help her decide. She lowered her window and settled into the mix of wind, jasmine, exhaust, and car horns. The streets were filled with similar hues of blue, grey, and brown suits, as Midtown emptied out on a Thursday afternoon. Her car halted at the next corner and she could overhear a woman cooing over her friend's new engagement ring. They both wore their hair pulled back in studded hair clips, their silk crème blouses tucked neatly inside their skirts and their suit jackets draped carefully over their shoulders like a cape, their friendship affirmed sartorially. Even though they didn't see her, Lily untucked her own white collared shirt and released her hair band. Her curly black hair began to frizz. "I'm looking forward to taking a break from work for a while," said the engaged woman. Her friend cast a forlorn look of envy. "I did promise Jared I would cook at least once a week, though. That will take some getting used to."

"You're very lucky," her friend responded.

Lily never thought she would quit working by choice, let alone, involuntarily. She needed to get out of midtown, away from its traffic and its fully employed residents. She recalled having a similar conversation with Brett, a guy she had dated officially for two months, but only saw four times. He had worked with Gabe at Buffalo Steers, but his expertise in restructuring finance had kept him secure, until it became clear no amount of restructuring would save the company. Given that he knew this before everyone else, he had found another position at the rival Bull Moose for a ten percent increase in salary. He had asked her to toast this accomplishment with him, to which she responded they should no longer see each other. Although she should've ended it on their third date, when he described his vision of a wife and four kids living in the brownstone next to his parents on 88th and Madison, but she believed in second chances.

She made her way to 2nd Avenue. She hadn't been to the Village since her New York University days, but it was still as familiar to her as it had been then. Marshall, the homeless chess player, still challenged passers-by outside Veselka. She had gained 12 pounds from the pierogis she ate during her first winter in New York and never won a single match. The Korean barbeque restaurant-by-early-evening and late-night karaoke bar displayed the remnants of the previous night's revelry on its windowsills.

She quickly pulled into the trucks and service lane on 14th street, scribbled "Be Back in 1 minute" on a piece of paper, secured it to her windshield, and burst into the NYU student center. She could smell the chicken already. She flashed her old student ID at the security officer and ran down the escalator to the Chick N' Bik kiosk in the back of the room.

"Six chicken and biscuits with that secret cheese sauce please." She scooped the to-go bag and ran back to the car, which was now blocked in by a sanitation truck and the City Bus. She grabbed the parking ticket off her windshield, hopped back into the car and devoured her first biscuit. The crispy fried skin smothered with the creamy, tangy cheese sauce melted in her mouth. She was on her third biscuit before she noticed the City Bus honking its horn. She quickly wiped off the sauce that had trickled down the side of her mouth.

With one hand she maneuvered the car out of the spot, while the other hand fed her the remaining three biscuits. Her stomach pushed at the seams of her fitted skirt. The brief moment of satisfaction soon gave way to guilt. She imagined the cholesterol filling her arteries. Despite her slim build and 30 years of age, she was three cheeseburgers away from a prescription. She cruised down Sixth Street, while Indian men hollered into their cell phones in an unfamiliar language with intermittent bouts of English in anticipation of dinner service. They smoked cigarettes, leaning against parking meters they had just bagged with "no parking signs" designed to mimic the official city ones. But the added adjective "no such parking" gave them away. During her brief vegetarian phase at Gabe's insistence, Indian food had been her staple, and East 6th street was her grocery store before it was replaced by a grocery that sold $5 apples. She reached the corner of 1st Ave and 7th street and slid into another reserved vehicle spot. She replaced her sign on the windshield and walked up to her college apartment building.

Velour green curtains now hung in the window where she had hung thrift store blinds. The stoop looked shiny and smelled of rosemary from potted plants, the trash can and recycling bins were emptied, and the iron rail was repainted to a solid black, all suggesting that it was someone's job to keep the place clean. She had thought the place had looked more beautiful before, with its discolored bricks, rattling wooden shutters, and mismatched trash cans, the way an old, weathered building evinces its indestructible nature. Now it looked as if it could crumple at a fallen tree branch.

Lily returned to her car and tossed the second parking ticket into her bag. She rolled up the window, turned up the radio station, and continued to circle the island.

National Public Radio now is live from Lynchburg, Virginia where Ramal Cady, the Democratic Presidential nominee, will be speaking shortly.

She hesitated at the thought of working for Cady. Would she fit in? Something about those overjoyous Cady campaign workers reminded her of the Seventh Day Adventists who had canvassed her childhood neighborhood soliciting donations and support. Her father had politely explained they did not believe in any religion, which fueled their passion even more.

We need change in America. And change doesn't come from Washington; it comes to Washington.

"Yes, we do. I need change, too," she mumbled to herself. She feared she would sprout roots in the basement if she stayed any longer. Cady had an ethereal way with words. It made the crowds swoon at his feet or lifted others to an imaginary place above ground. He could make a mother loan her kids for a scientific experiment.

Cady then began to rattle off a list of issues that must be changed, the War, Healthcare, Education, Energy, etc., the same issues she had heard repeatedly over the years. Yet, this time he was *supposed* to be different. Good luck, she thought. And besides, *how* was he going to do it? She never thought he had outlined this clearly enough. Uproarious clapping constantly interrupted his speeches. He just had to say two words, like "Green Jobs," and the crowd erupted. This time, he paused longer than usual.

Change won't come easy. The crowd shouted no. *All of you will need to help remake America.* The crowd chanted "Yes!" in unison. *The road will be long and arduous, but no one, not even the President of the United States, can do it alone.* "No!" No, he can't, Lily thought. *I'm asking each one of you to play your individual role so that collectively we can succeed as a nation.* The crowd began to chant Ready for Cady!" What was her role? Lily wondered. *I'm asking you to join me in bringing change to America.* But how? How could she? *Focusing your life solely on making a buck shows a certain poverty of ambition. It asks too little of yourself.* Go on… *Because it's only when you hitch your wagon to something larger than yourself that you realize your true potential.* The crowd roared.

She repeated the words in her head. "It's only when you hitch your wagon to something larger than yourself that you realize your true potential." Sailboats and kayaks danced above the bright Hudson as she whizzed up the West Side Highway. She felt lighter than she had felt in a long time, like she could float through air. She yearned to disappear into the car speakers and be as close to Cady's voice as possible. Heels and Ellsworth wasn't larger than herself. It was just another mark on her top-ten list of employers. She applied to college based on a top-ten list. She applied to law school based on another top-ten list. She had been a plane on autopilot her whole life. Cady's campaign was out there in the real world charting a new flight plan.

"On to Harlem." A resounding certainty escaped her mouth for the first time. She would apply for a job with Ramal Cady's campaign. Sure, it may have been a while since she dabbled in politics, but her experience certainly rivaled those who spent their afternoons canvassing tourists while wearing silk screened Cady t-shirts and tattoos. She had voted in three previous Presidential elections. With one hand on the wheel, the other rummaged through her tote bag and found a copy of her resume. It was marked up with edits, but Cady wouldn't care if she brought change to America with a marred resume. Soon she was in Harlem, and as she whirled down 125th street she made a mental note to catch a show at the Apollo one night after work. Maybe she could find a cheap studio sublet here, something she could afford on a campaigner's salary. She would visit the Studio Museum during her lunch hour or savor the barbecue at Dinosaur restaurant. Harlem's tree-lined brownstones would be a wonderful contrast to the skyscrapers of midtown. She lurched to a stop in front of a stone building with no address and bearing a poster of Cady's face gazing over the horizon. It was affixed by masking tape to the inside door. For the third time, she placed her makeshift sign on her windshield and went inside.

The office gleamed with new laptop computers, cell phone chargers laid in an orderly fashion across a bookshelf; not a single piece of paper in sight. Wall sized campaign posters loomed from three walls beckoning her to *Be The Change*. Despite the untucked blouse and the frizz of her hair, she was overdressed. A young lady in jeans and Cady t-shirt typed furiously on the computer at the main desk and another similarly dressed guy mimicked her movements at a small desk in the corner. They both looked 18. And neither noticed her arrival. Lily leaned over the counter.

"Can I help you?" asked the young lady. She didn't look like an ordinary receptionist, the type that her law firm usually hired. She had short hair and unkempt nails. Lily suddenly felt unsure.

The young lady asked again, "Excuse me?"

"Yes. I'm here to apply for a job." She was committed to the cause. She certainly didn't want the other side to win. They had done enough damage already.

"What kind of job?" This time the guy glanced up at her, shrugged to his colleague, and returned to clicking on his computer. What were they typing about?

"Any kind." The lady broke away from the computer and assessed Lily's suit.

Lily couldn't tell if the girl's smile was really a smirk. "Can you email me your resume?"

"I have a copy right here."

She didn't flinch. "We only use email. I need to send it to RC's office in Denver right away."

"Oh." When she interned for Representative Weissman she had to provide her resume and references on parchment. "RC?"

"RC. Ramal Cady. You do know what you're applying for, right?" asked the lady.

"Of course." RC flowed easily off the tongue, like POTUS. She liked it.

"I can scan it," the guy volunteered. His smile appeared genuine and he rushed off to the back room.

The lady returned to her typing. The guy returned to his computer. And they all three sat in silence.

"Would you like me to wait? Do you need a cover letter or transcript?"

"No. They will call you," she said and continued typing.

"Who are 'they'?"

"Denver," they both replied in unison. Only then did Lily realize that the two of them had been typing Gmail-chats with each other.

This time when she returned to her car there was no parking ticket. Third time is definitely a charm, even when violating the parking codes. Traffic inched back to the George Washington Bridge, which provided her with plenty of time to wonder what she would do if she were rejected for this job. Maybe she should drive over to the Brooklyn Bridge so she could just toy with the idea of hopelessness. Her phone vibrated from an unknown number. She answered.

"Hello?"

"Hi, is this Lillian DeMarco?" The caller had pronounced the name correctly.

"Yes. It's Lily. Who's this?"

"This is Alex calling from Davis Wright's office. You applied to work on RC's campaign?"

"That was fast."

"We do move quickly here."

"I'm just down the street. I can come by for an interview right now."

"I'm calling from Denver. Hold on a sec." Lily could hear Alex mumbling over the phone.

"Do you have a car?"

"Excuse me?

"Do you have a car?"

"No, well, yes, but I share it with my Dad. What is the car for?"

"Lily, I just need to know whether you can get a car."

"Sure, um — yes, I can." Her dad would enjoy making a car-sharing schedule. He would have a spreadsheet broken down by 30-minute timeslots. But perhaps RC's office didn't realize how frequently taxis moved in New York.

"Do you believe in RC?"

"Yes. I want him to win. It's time to end the war. Get healthcare for all. Reinforce the EPA regulations. Also, I've voted Democrat every time, except that one time for Mayor when—"

"Lily, do you believe in RC?" he asked again. Perhaps her cell phone reception had died momentarily.

"Yes. Sure."

"Great. You're assigned to Georgia. What's your email address? I'll send you the info."

She sat silent and confused.

"Lily?"

"I thought I applied to the New York office."

"Oh, that's just a recruiting office. We are sending people all over the country to the premiere battleground states."

"Is there something I can do in New York?"

"No."

"Where in Georgia?

"You'll show up to the Atlanta Headquarters and they'll tell you your location."

"Why Georgia?"

"Georgia is the new Ohio."

Now that was definitely surprising. She couldn't recall any election being decided by the electoral count in Georgia, unlike Ohio or Florida, which alone determined the rest of the country's future. In fact, she didn't think any candidate had even bothered to campaign in Georgia. "Really?"

"Oh yes. We have our sights set on taking Georgia and you will be part of history when we do!"

"What will I be doing?"

"They will tell you when you get there."

"When do I get there?"

"Sunday."

"But it's Thursday."

"Like I said, we move fast here."

"Umm." She hesitated. Could she really move down there so quickly? But then again, she was unemployed and Jerry was living in her fully furnished apartment. All she needed was to pack a suitcase or two. This would definitely pose a challenge to any car share schedule her father could devise.

"Lily, we could definitely use someone with your experience. It's hard work. Field. But you will be highly valued on this campaign. We don't have many people with graduate degrees and previous work experience on the ground." That somehow didn't surprise her.

"Don't be mistaken, Georgia is an honor. Ford DeJeune has put together one of the best teams in any state down there." She would be valued. She would be busy bringing change to America rather than reading about it on six different websites every day.

"Can I let you know tomorrow?"

"Sorry, but no. Like I said, things move quickly. I need an answer. We have people begging to be a part of our staff. I can't make any promises, but with your experience I'll bet that you will be offered a Regional Field Director position ... and those aren't easy to come by. And, um, Lily?"

"Yes?"

"You'll play a role in the most important history-making event that America has ever experienced." Perhaps this is why she felt she was living a slow death. She hadn't done anything useful in two months, other than help her mother repaint the kitchen. The closest she'd been to history was when it was forced upon her during 9-11, and she was stuck underground on the subway the entire time, helpless.

"OK."

"OK. What?"

"I'm in."

"That's great. So the pay is $2000 a month with benefits; $2500 if Ford offers you an RFD slot. I'll email you the info." With that, Alex was gone too.

"Two thousand dollars a month! Don't you earn more in unemployment?" Gabe asked as she drove back to Paterson, balancing her phone on her lap.

"I really need to get one of those wireless gadgets."

"Bluetooth. What about Pennsylvania? Don't they have an operation here?"

"I guess it's already filled."

"Right, because who wants to go to freaking Georgia?" Gabe didn't sound convinced. "There are no Italians below the Mason-Dixon line."

"Can you help me buy a car?"

"What do you need a car for?"

"It's Georgia, Gabe, I need a car. Do you still have your old Volvo for sale?"

"You're headed to the South. You need a Chevy or a Dodge."

"Gabe!"

"Ok. It's $2000. The amount of your first month's earnings."

"I'll take it."

"And Lil, I am excited for your adventure. It makes my move to the Pennsylvania farmland seem like a subway ride to Century 21."

"I ran into Naomi Ellis today."

"She looks the same, doesn't she?"

"Even better."

"I need to find out her secret."

"The thing is she was going on about her life since high school, her beautiful kids, her husband and I realized I had nothing to report. It's not that I wanted to talk about the exact same things; it's just I had nothing to say. Nothing."

"That'll soon change."

"I hope so."

"Are you Crazy?!" He shouted into the phone.

"Don't start with that ridiculous cattle call."

"Are you Ready?!"

"I may be a staffer now, but I refuse to noodle the crowd that way."

"Are you crazy ready for Cady?!" His voice boomed from the speaker, drowning out the background radio. She sat silent.

"I'm only asking one more time. Are you—"

"Ok. Ok. I'm Cady Crazy Ready!"

CHAPTER 2

Rita was very pleased with the news of Lily's move. She had drafted plans to renovate the basement's bedroom and mini-kitchen, which she could now implement. She also found her old *Taste of the South* magazines containing the best recipes for fried chicken and collard greens, alligator rolls and crawfish étouffée. She constructed a recipe box out of an old leather handbag and hatbox. Meanwhile Rick, while happy his daughter was employed, had several more questions.

"I don't understand. They want you there on Sunday? That doesn't give you any time to find a place to live."

"Rick, there are plenty of motels that rent rooms by the week."

"I got an email saying they will find me housing." Lily said.

"What exactly will you be doing?"

"Field."

"Don't you need training?"

"Rick, field is meeting people. Traveling. Not being stuck behind a computer."

"I'm 30 years-old. I think I can figure this out."

"Well, let me see your road map."

With Rick's markings overlaid on the road atlas, she was fully prepared to make the 879-mile trek to Atlanta. She had taken the train to Philadelphia to meet Gabe, who had sold her his old car and gave her a used guidebook to the South that only covered the Mid-Atlantic States. "Never thought I'd head to the Deep South." She drove the car back to Northern New Jersey, where she quickly packed her things and showed her father on Google Earth the exact address of the Atlanta office and its surrounding streets. She packed the departing gifts of mosquito repellant and a copy of *Southern Accents and Architecture* from her mother. Even Jerry had called her immediately upon receiving her email that she would be in Georgia until November.

"I will buy your apartment."

"I know Jerry, but I don't want to sell."

"Ok then. Do not go OTP."

"Huh?"

"Outside the Perimeter. I taught a class at Georgia Tech once. Be sure to stay inside."

Within 18 hours she was driving south on 1-95. She located the NPR station in Delaware and settled into the political punditry. *Small business,* a pundit explained, *is the heart of America. Whichever candidate can win the heartland will win the General Election.* Rick was a small business owner. He had been a copywriter, and rather than work on Madison Avenue, he remained in Paterson and started his own advertising business creating ads for local car dealerships, restaurants, beauty parlors, and grocers. Beauty triumphed over brains, he had reluctantly explained to her once, because beauty sold. Lily thought this was why the slim, petite women anchored the news, while the tall, athletic ones were off reporting from Iraq.

What will be the effect of this long primary on the election? The fact that she had a job. *Bill Ryan, one of the candidates who was defeated in the primary now joins us from…* She turned up the radio. Ryan's affair with a campaign staffer had accelerated his own demise, but he had a loyal following which pundits now referred to as the Ryan Democrats. Regardless of his infidelity, Lily still found him charming. *Make no mistake. This is the best-organized campaign machine I have ever seen. Never in the history of Democratic politics has there been a campaign so well organized. After all, it beat me, didn't it?'* Yes it did. And despite her doubts of Cady's chances at fixing all the ills in the world, she was going to help win Georgia.

Lily pulled off the interstate to circle Washington D.C., a city she hadn't seen since her internship interview. The Jefferson Memorial came into view, and she recalled her seventh grade civics field trip, when her crush on Bobby Rader outshined any monument. It was the main reason she had convinced her parents to withdraw from their savings account to pay for it. She had worn a pale blue scarf and a matching beret in the hopes he would pass a note on the bus ride, "Will you be my girlfriend? Check Yes, No, or Maybe." She would've checked "Yes" and they would've held hands as they strolled along the National Mall discussing the Declaration of Independence, sipping their Pepsis, and dining from a hot dog cart at lunch. But that hadn't happened. He had bought her a Pepsi after he accidentally knocked hers out of her hands and onto that scarf and cap. She hadn't had many relationships. None in high school. She didn't need one. She had had Gabe. And just the one in college. She was whom romantic advice columnists referred to as a "late bloomer." She never understood why it was disparaging to peak later in life. Sure some girls peaked at 16, but she liked her chances better if she peaked at 32. She had two more years.

She parked on a side street, just east of the Washington Monument. The polished buildings of the Smithsonian loomed in the dusk behind her. The streets were sprinkled lightly with pedestrians, mainly tourists. They were quieter and more subdued than the streets of New York would be at this hour. "If Cady wins, maybe I could move here," she thought. Jerry had offered her an all cash payment for the apartment. Returning to New York no longer held the same appeal it once had. She strolled down Pennsylvania Avenue towards the White House. This time she didn't need Bobby Rader to enjoy the D.C sights, just her trusty used Volvo and the guidebook Gabe donated along with it. The sidewalks emptied as she drew closer, not a tourist in sight. Apparently the White House fascinated no one, except for a handful of war protestors. She peered through the iron gates onto the south lawn, squeezing her nose and cheeks as far they could go. The iron felt refreshingly cool against her face. The White House gleamed under the light of the night sky. She stood as high as she could on her tiptoes feeling excited and yet nervous at what lay before her. She felt ten years younger and overwhelmed by an unfamiliar sense of wonderment. Where *would* she sleep next? Is Georgia as hot as people say it is? Were there others like her?

The Washingtonian suburban sprawl quickly gave way to green sylvan hills: Virginia. She had never traveled this far south, but found the landscape oddly comforting. The highway, now lined with trees, grew wider and quieter. Cars quickened their speed as the limit increased to 75 mph. Billboards advertising cigarettes, church, NASCAR, and beef dotted the highway. A few remained blank except for a 1-800 number for potential advertisers. She rolled down her window and breathed in the early summer air, which had a coolness that smelled of sweet tobacco leaves. Suddenly, she was ravenous and spotted a sign for Richmond.

"The heart of the Confederacy. We should've switched out the license plate before you left." She found Gabe's periodic calls on the drive supportive.

"It's 2008. No one identifies themselves as a Confederate."

"Have you not heard of Civil War reenactments?"

"Did I do the right thing?"

"Getting out of Rick and Rita's basement, yes. Georgia, only time will tell. But then again, what do I know? I'm relegated to a farm in Pennsylvania."

"Promise me you'll join a local Gay Farmer's association."

"No. The nearest one is in California. Call me if you run into any Rebels."

She exited to a truck stop, where the gas station linked to a fast food chain. There was a diner attached to the rear of the building. It had four empty stools at the counter. "Diner's closed," said the cashier when she walked in. "Only food is at Taco Queen." The cashier pointed to a teenager behind the taco assembly line. He grinned widely and proudly showcased to her the two different tortillas, corn and flour, eager to make even one taco. The dried meat and brown lettuce wouldn't have been appealing even during a stress binge. She surveyed the place for something other than packaged potato chips and beef jerky. She wanted to begin her southern stint with cleaner arteries. She opted for diet cola and a loaf of bread.

"We've got some pretty sights here in Richmond," said the cashier, as if the word "tourist" were stamped on Lily's head.

"Well, I'm sort of in a rush. Need to be in Atlanta by tomorrow."

The cashier scowled, as if she had already heard the same sentiment 20 times today. "The Jeffersonian Capitol Building and The Jefferson Davis House are just down the road."

"Oh. I actually just saw the Jefferson Memorial," Lily said politely.

"Different Jefferson," the cashier sternly responded. Lily suddenly recalled her eighth grade lecture on the Civil War when Jefferson Davis was elected as the President of the Confederacy. She had no idea people memorialized him as an actual President.

She quickly returned to her car and hastened her speed, determined to make it a few more hours before resting at a cheap motel, yet another new experience for her. She would eat out of the vending machine and brew instant coffee from the bathroom sink faucet. The road ahead was dark aside from the occasional glimmer of a 24-hour fast food restaurant sign. She drove with the brights on, which illuminated the outline of the thick trees towering the highways. Only she and a handful of trucks occupied the road. The black sky, with its sprinkling of stars, stretched for miles. And although she was driving, she felt soothed by a stillness that usually escaped her. Even with the radio turned down low, so that the fiddle of the late night bluegrass music faded into the background, it took four rings to hear her phone.

"Ah hello?"

"Hello, Lily. This is Ford from Georgia."

"Oh yes, hi! I'm really excited to—" she began.

"I just wanted to remind you that you are expected in Atlanta tomorrow morning at 9 a.m. I'll see you then." He hung up before she had a chance to respond. There was an irksome similarity between Ford and her previous boss at Heels and Ellsworth. Mr. Davies had been indifferent to any small talk. She grew concerned about working for Ford, but shrugged it off. It was the Cady campaign after all. Ford was trying to be part of history just like her. She struggled to drive for another two hours before surrendering to exhaustion at a roadside motel somewhere in rural South Carolina. Yet, she couldn't fall asleep. She drew the window shades to block out the neon light from the "Pink Pony" across the street, but they only closed half way. She laid extra towels over the sheets to buffer the loose mattress springs. She still couldn't sleep. She checked her Blackberry, a nervous habit when she didn't know what to anticipate the next day at work. One email from Rick explaining that unlike New Jersey, gas stations were only self-serve in Georgia, and one from Jerry asking if he could have a small party with a rented chef from "Behind the Kitchen." She quickly responded "Thanks" and "Yes" and then rolled the bed pillow and hugged it tightly.

***

The next morning, she arrived at Atlanta Headquarters promptly at 9 a.m., only to be surprised that her future was housed at an old medical facility. The parking lot was empty, the door was locked, and a tattered sign *Be the Change* hung loosely on the front door. Lily followed the "Patients Enter Around Back" sign but the back door was locked as well. Ford didn't answer his phone. Perhaps this was just an outpost? Sweat puddles formed underneath her suit. Apparently, this was May in Georgia.

A used station wagon lurched into the parking lot, blaring punk rock music. The car eased into the parking space next to Lily. It displayed two bumper stickers. One of Cady's and the other read "Hell is a Flinching Lion." To Lily's surprise, a petite woman emerged from the car, dressed in jeans and a flowered tank top.

"Yo," she said as she peered from the top of her sunglasses.

"Hey. I'm Lily." She couldn't help being nervous.

"Great." The woman opened up the rear door and dragged out a large box. Lily noticed the taut muscle of her arm bulging under a simple tattoo. She couldn't make out the rectangular shape.

"Do you need some help?"

"Nah." She set the box down, leaned against the locked front door, and lit up a cigarette. The air-conditioned haven of the office would have to wait.

"I guess everyone is late today," Lily commented. Other than their two cars, the parking lot was empty. There was not even a car on the road. The modern Atlanta skyline showcased glass buildings that seemed to sprout from trees. It was dotted with flashing billboards, across rolling hills. Yet, the city stood eerily quiet.

Her nameless companion inhaled the smoke, holding her breath for nearly a full minute, and then exhaled into perfect quarter sized smoke rings. "Nah. It's Sunday. Don't get started until noon. Church morning."

Church morning? She hadn't heard anyone utter those words since the 9th grade. "Oh. I thought I was supposed to be here at 9?"

"Did Ford tell you that? He says that to everyone." Now Lily yearned for a cigarette, even though she didn't smoke.

"By the way, what's your name?"

The girl put out the cigarette butt against the concrete siding and flicked it into the trashcan five yards away. "Rachel," she replied.

"That's an interesting tattoo. What's it of?"

Rachel scooped up the box in one hand, unlocked the door with the left, and peered one last time over her sunglasses. "Georgia," she replied and strolled into the building. Lily smiled and followed quickly behind. She pushed out of her mind the anxious look on her dad's face, her New York apartment, and the skyscrapers looming behind her as she drove across the George Washington Bridge. *Georgia, I'm ready.* She whispered to herself.

CHAPTER 3

The first thing she noticed was the cheeseburger wrapper that stuck to her shoe. The dregs of day old diced onions became lodged in the creases of her soles. She nearly stumbled upon an overflowing trashcan placed beside the door as a reminder for someone to empty it. The room was wide, but unusually dark for an early summer morning. Lily didn't find any windows. The musty smell suggested no path for fresh air. There were laptops propped on card tables and two people tucked inside sleeping bags lying underneath. Another person snored heavily on the couch. The cheeseburger wrapper was not alone; to-go bags from every fast food outlet littered the edges of the room, along with a few empty beer bottles. Campaign signs tacked to the wall resembled finger paintings by children rather than a printed glossy. The entire room looked more like a prison library than the nerve center of the "best organized campaign machine in history." She could only imagine what the Alabama office looked like.

Rachel signaled to Lily to find a chair, sidestepped the clutter with ease, and marched back to her office without acknowledging anyone. Lily made room for herself amidst the disarray to wait. She hated to wait. More time to reflect upon her decision. She'd rather just be busy. Although the drive was tedious, now to be here, in this musty dungeon, amidst fast food wrappers, she fought against the impulse to get back in the car and head north on I-85. The two sleeping bag inhabitants murmured as they squirmed around together. This must be how caterpillars mate. The snorer occasionally woke himself with his own sound but then immediately fell back to sleep. His t-shirt barely covered his bulging belly and the layer of dirt on his jeans no longer appeared washable. His flip-flops exposed deep callouses and corns on his toes, and his wrinkled forehead made him look older than her father. A half empty bottle of whiskey nested in the pocket of his underarm. She bit her lip.

A tall, thin, striking blonde, glided through the front door. She instantly noticed Lily just as Lily instantly noticed her, although the blonde was the kind who was instantly noticeable. Even if Lily had spent the five extra minutes this morning to blush her pale cheeks and find her lipstick that was buried somewhere in the bottom of her bag, she still wouldn't be nearly as noticeable. She pulled her brown frizz back into a hair clip. The blonde floated across the room without any trash interference. Her Cady t-shirt fitted perfectly around the contours of her body, suggesting it was tailor made, unlike the usual bagginess of mass-produced t-shirts. Lily smoothed her skirt and jacket. She needed to buy her own Cady t-shirt.

"Welcome, I'm Gianna." Her voice was a soft raspy purr, which reminded Lily of a host of a late night long distance love song dedication radio show. Lily shook her welcoming hand, which felt at smooth as silk. Not a single red splotch on her face; the only red was on her outlined lips. She had the perfect button nose, the kind Lily had only seen in celebrity gossip magazines. But those were likely doctored, and nothing about Gianna looked faked. She looked as if she only shopped at department stores, not a discount online retailer.

"Lily." She said forcefully and a little too loudly. Gianna flinched in response and then noted a check on her clipboard. She asked Lily if she could help Sam and Parker, the two young sleeping-baggers, to prepare for today's meeting. Lily nodded and stood up as the two of them surfaced. The guy's thick curly black hair nearly engulfed his head, and the rectangle shaped glasses overshadowed his blue eyes. He jumped up to meet Lily. He wore a Boston University t-shirt and Cady cap.

"Hi. Lily you said?" She nodded. "I'm Sam and this is Parker." Parker joined him at his side, and his arms instinctively circled her waist. He was just a couple of inches taller than she. She beamed at him, and he kissed her forehead in return.

"It's nice to meet you," Parker smiled at Lily. Her smooth, long blonde hair showed no signs of bed-head, and her buttoned Cady polo, which sported the campaign insignia instead of the horse, bore no wrinkles. Camping indoors suited her.

Piles of papers were laid out on the table before them ready to be copied, sorted, and stapled, similar to assembling loan documents at the firm, except that the firm had an air-conditioned conference room and catered lunch. The click of the stapler reminded her of her own utility. It had been a while. The front page of the packet was titled "Organizer Training" and displayed the Cady logo of a rising white sun against a blue sky and red and white striped landscape. By now it was nearly as recognizable as the American flag. Lily flipped through the pages and noticed a few misspellings and typos, as if someone had just typed it out the night before.

"Should we correct these?" she asked.

Both Sam and Parker looked confused by the question, but replied "No" in unison, and resumed their conversation.

"What state were you in during the Primary?" Parker asked. "We were in Tex-ahs." She playfully attempted the Texas accent, but Lily still bit her lip to prevent herself from correcting the grammar.

"We spint ar dayz canvassing and nahts playing gee-tar." Sam chimed in with his own version. She would fail miserably if speaking in local accents were a job requirement.

"I actually didn't work in the primary."

"You didn't?" They responded again in unison.

"I've worked in politics before. Just a while back." She also wouldn't reveal she had been an intern.

"I've never worked in politics before. Cady's the first person I voted for," said Parker and resumed her stapling. "I'm thrilled to be here. My family and I usually go to the Vineyard on summer breaks, but I couldn't ask for a better graduation gift than working on this campaign." Lily hoped she meant graduation from a graduate school. Even a Masters in culinary arts.

"Yeah. Some of my buddies are interning at Goldbank before they start their MBAs but this is going to be way more important." Sam said.

"What about you?" Parker asked Lily. "What are you missing out on this summer?" Endlessly staring at her laptop computer screen, aimlessly window shopping the malls of Paterson, New Jersey, and serving as her mother's subcontractor. Nothing with a ten-week expiration date. She fumbled for an answer.

"Well, the usual summertime New York activities. Weekends at the beach. Concerts in Central Park. But yes, this is much more important."

"It's so worth it, though." Sam agreed. "New York will always be there." Would it? She wondered. She wasn't so sure anymore. She didn't have a job. Jerry had offered cash for the apartment. Her best friend now lived on a farm.

"Oh, Cady has to win. Otherwise I really will move to Paris." responded Parker. She looked sincere and it reminded Lily of the time she suggested the same thing about Canada at the thought of Gregg Burns getting re-elected.

"It'll be London for me," chimed Gianna.

Lily watched the three of them plot their Plan B lives on the chance that Cady didn't win. She didn't want to confess that this was her Plan B guided by a binge meal of chicken biscuits and Cady's political-moral suasion. Her immediate plan was to scrape the onions out from the soles of her shoes.

"I love to walk into an office to see busy campaign workers!" A voice boomed from the doorway. *This must be*

Ford. Lily glanced at her watch. *11:30.* Hmph. Gianna sidled up to his side, handing him the clipboard. She brushed a speck of dirt off his forehead and lingered closely beside him. Next to her, Ford was short and a bit stubby, but he spoke confidently and seemed unaffected by the Georgia heat in his argyle sweater vest over a crisp white collared shirt and khakis. He wore a gold Cady campaign insignia lapel pin.

"You must be Lily." He walked with the kind of pace she hadn't seen since she entered Virginia. Short and quick.

"Hi." He took her arm, instead of her hand, a style she had seen work so well for President Stafford. His caramel-brown skin and brown eyes appeared warm and inviting, but his formal mannerism was off-putting.

"Lily, I was going to wait until the meeting to let you know of your assignment, but I'll do you a favor and let you know now. You will be the Regional Field Director for the Northeast Region of Georgia." She had no idea what that meant. Northeast still signified the New York-New Jersey corridor to her.

"Ok. Do I need to do anything before the meeting?"

"Nope." Lily wasn't sure then why knowing now was better than knowing in an hour, but she played along.

"We are going to brunch at Trois, a fantastic French Bistro right here in Atlanta before the meeting. Would you like to join?" Even though Ford's words meant to be helpful, his tone made her feel 10 years old. She glanced at Gianna whose once welcoming nature had disappeared. Sam and Parker simply gazed at each other.

"That's ok. I ate already." She was starving, but also intimidated by the foursome, and being a fifth wheel was worse than grabbing lunch alone. Gianna tucked her arm underneath Ford's and they strolled out the door, with Sam and Parker trailing behind, holding hands. She felt a pang of envy. She wished she had someone to hold her hand. She sank back into the chair. Her car was parked just outside. Living on Gabe's farm in Pennsylvania could be Plan C. She eyed a half-eaten fried chicken sandwich on the table beside the snorer with the Evan Williams bottle. He had left to get coffee and donuts.

"Are they gone?" Rachel shouted from the doorway.

"Yes."

"Great. Now we can get to work. Want to help?"

CHAPTER 4

Rachel's office resembled a hovel, which she kept dark, except for the glow from a single desk lamp. It reeked of cigarettes. A potpourri of toiletries lay atop a mini refrigerator and a towel hung from a nail above. Three cartons of cigarettes lay in the other corner. Mounds of paper surrounded the two laptops on the desk. Billboard sized posters of Martin Luther King Jr., Gandhi, and Ramal Cady decorated the walls. Inspiring, but all except Cady had been assassinated. Books lay in a pile on the edge of her desk. *Weary Feet, Rested Souls, Born in Calhoun, The Children*, and others. Books she'd never heard of.

"Take a seat." Lily followed Rachel's lead and shoved the paper on her chair to the floor and settled in. Rachel fiddled with a cigarette in one hand while she sipped straight black coffee in the other. "My ex-husband used to hate when I played with my cigarette. Smoking was ok. Playing was not."

"You were married?" She instantly regretted the way that sounded and began to backpedal. "I mean you look young." Not a hint of a wrinkle. An amazing feat for someone who could blow smoke into double rings. They reminded Lily of her bubble gum blowing contests with Gabe as kids. He always won by blowing a bubble inside another one.

"We got married right after college. Grew apart I suppose. We're not technically divorced yet. Been separated since the primary. He thinks I chose Cady over him. Campaign work is tough." She pulled out a Tupperware box from under her desk "Cookie? It's vegan."

Lily yearned to pry into the break-up, but for the moment held off. "Thanks." She took two.

"I don't want to eat anything that's been killed."

"But you smoke?"

"Yes, I'd rather kill myself with cigarettes than eat something killed." Her smile indicated that she wasn't even afraid of death. "So here's what we've got to do. We have a big statewide meeting this afternoon and…" Rachel hurriedly explained the various tasks of collating different documents. She paced as she spoke, which forced her to walk in circles around the office about eight times before she came to a pause. At which point she grabbed another cookie and then continued for another eight circles. Lily felt tired. Finally, she stopped to hand over some documents, which they began to collate and bind.

"Did you travel to all the states during the primary?"

"Fourteen of them. Pennsylvania, Oregon, West Virginia, South Carolina were my favorite. Nice excuse to see the country."

"That must've been exciting. I just watched the results on television."

"I don't own a TV."

Lily realized she forgot to pack her own TV, an old 20 inch buried in the hall closet blocked by David's snowboard.

"It was lots of fun," Rachel continued. "Reason why I knew I could no longer be married."

"Did you meet someone new?"

"Hmm. There was John in Oregon, Chuck in West Virginia, Anton in South Carolina, Carlos in Texas," She grinned.

She admired the shamelessness. She barely mustered up the nerve to ask someone out on a date.

"So why the tattoo of Georgia? Are you from here?"

"Nope. Vermont."

"I'm from New Jersey."

"They wanted to send me to Ohio, but I chose Georgia."

"Why?" Rachel reached into the corner and tossed a book. "Catch." She missed.

"Born in Calhoun?"

"Read it." Lily glanced at the back cover and recognized Lamar Lovell, the Congressman from Georgia and civil rights hero.

"That was the 1950s, though, over 50 years ago." Rachel ignored her comment.

"So what inspired you to come on board?" asked Rachel.

"I worked in politics a while back." She trusted Rachel enough to hint her true age. "Actually interned for my Congresswoman during Stafford's second term."

"Oh yeah? You're an old timer like me." Lily smiled in return, but her stomach felt queasy. "What have you been doing since?"

"Law school." Rachel nodded as if she expected that answer. "Big firm. And well, that work is drying up."

"SUVs and mortgage-backed securities. Who would've thought at the same time. Let's keep our ages between us." She pointed toward the main room. Lily agreed.

Lily thumbed through Lovell's memoir while Rachel put the finishing touches on her power point presentation. She enjoyed this quiet spell of productivity. But it was quickly interrupted by Ford, Sam, and Parker returning from lunch.

"Lily, speak to you in the hallway?" Ford asked, poking his head through the door, as if afraid to step completely inside. Lily glanced at Rachel who nodded. She couldn't figure out which one was her boss. Ford then indicated for her, Sam, and Parker to form a huddle.

"The three of you will be working together in Ludlow, Georgia," he informed her and the sleeping bag twins.

"But we just rented a place in Buckhead!" Parker looked at Sam sheepishly.

"Ludlow?" Lily asked.

"Can't we at least be assigned the suburbs of Atlanta?" Sam asked Ford.

"Lily is in charge." Ford smiled and walked off, leaving the two of them to turn their pleading faces to Lily.

"Where is Ludlow?" she repeated.

Sam sighed. Parker shook her head in discouragement and then hugged Sam tightly. "We've been lucky so far. Only had the cities during the primary. We can do this."

Sam agreed and kissed her. Lily wished Rachel was coming to Ludlow with her, wherever that was. She was about to ask one last time, but Parker finally responded.

"Ludlow is rural Georgia. Foothills of the mountains."

Parker and Sam strolled back into the main room with their arms circled around each other and their heads rested against each other's shoulders.

CHAPTER 5

Cars overflowed with campaign materials, suitcases, and air mattresses, and uniformly sported Ramal Cady bumper stickers and out of state license plates, mostly from New York, Massachusetts, Vermont, California, and Connecticut. Over one hundred cars squeezed into every inch of the parking lot. Lily walked into the auditorium tentatively, her head ducked, as if she were crashing a charity ball without having donated. While she didn't know anyone in particular, everyone looked familiar. She had seen these organizers on television wading through the ruckus of the Iowa caucuses, drowning out the opposition by twenty decibels. They had squealed with such joy at a $5 contribution on the streets, making people feel like they had contributed $5000. They followed people five blocks, down the stairs, and into the subway to secure a pledge card support. She had found their efforts endearing; their loyalty to Cady unshaken by the mockery they received from passers-by. And now she was one of them. One of 100 Presidential campaign workers in Georgia, who had all joined forces for their statewide staff meeting at the downtown law offices of Talmadge Adair LLP, borrowed space from prominent donors to Cady's campaign. Yet, unlike Heels and Ellsworth, where she would have ridden the elevator up to a floor with a view and several secretaries, she was ushered by security into the basement auditorium. She searched the room for Rachel, Sam, or Parker. She spotted Gianna roaming about the room, greeting everyone with a double cheek kiss.

"Hey there!" A young man approached her wearing a nametag that read "Justin" in bright blue with a sketch of the Candidate's logo as the dot of the "i". He bore an excited face, unmarked by the mundane realities of buying groceries or mowing the lawn. "You're Lily," he announced as he squinted at her name tag. She didn't have the logo over her "i".

"Yes. Nice to meet you. Did you just get in town?"

"Yes, drove in from New Hampshire." She noticed his flip-flops and made a mental note to shop at a discount store later. He then rattled off the names of others in the room so fast, that by the time she could make them out, he was on to the next cluster of people. "They just got in from California. But they started as interns in Denver when Cady ran for Senate. How about you?"

"New York," she replied.

"Oh, then you must know those guys." He pointed to two guys hunkered behind their laptops in the corner. "Umm." He was discouraged by his momentary lapse in memory.

"I actually worked for Representative Weissman."

He thought long and hard and then shook his head "Don't know him."

"She. And it was couple of cycles ago." He was probably still in grade school at the time. She was about to explain she hadn't worked in the primary, but spotted Rachel on the side of the stage. "It was nice to meet you. I want to say hi to Rachel." He eagerly nodded, recognizing the urge to reunite.

As the room filled with more organizers, the smell of cigarettes, lingering alcohol, fast food grease, and lack of regular sleep or shower signaled campaign momentum. Together Rachel and Lily moved about the room as people flaunted opaque job titles: Faith Director, Youth Director, Assisted Living Outreach Director, Barber Shop and Beauty Shop Directors, Daycare Drop-off Director, Supermarket Cart

Volunteer Director. Lily tried to keep up, but she was never any good at remembering names upon a first introduction. The job titles might as well have been in Russian (she had studied French). She didn't want to disappoint Rachel, so she just nodded as they swiftly moved throughout the room, meeting nearly every one of the 100 staffers. Lily hoped there were an organizational chart and an employee directory.

Rachel confessed that a few titles of "Director" were handed out to those whose parents' companies contributed over $100,000 (in individual contributions of course).

"So is my title of Regional Field Director frivolous too?" Lily asked.

"Ultimately, we are all just community organizers." Rachel answered. "So you remember April, *the National Volunteer Director* in Denver?"

"No. I don't know the name."

"She used to sleep with Jacob Bing, the *National Field Director*. Before she became the Volunteer Director. Now she's with Jamie Collins who is the *National Political Director*, and he and Michael Sands, the current *National Deputy Field Director*, ran a political consulting firm, but before that they owned a real estate company on the outskirts of Denver. " Rachel took a quick breath and continued. "How about Sarah Stevens? Know her?"

Lily shook her head. The names blurred into each other. Did she really need to know who all these people were?

"Sarah Stevens, now the *Finance Director*, raised nearly 3 million dollars alone for Cady and she's married to David Stevens, CEO of WestBank, who used to work for her father when he ran MidWest Bank, before he ran for Governor of Colorado and got beat in the primary by the ex-Governor, who then served as an adviser to Cady's Senate campaign four years ago." Lily did recognize MidWest Bank.

As they roamed the room, Rachel also recognized many people she had worked with before. At each introduction, they asked Lily where she was during the primary and why she joined the campaign. By now her answers were crisp: (1) New

York, and (2) return to work in politics. When she asked others the same "Why" question, she got: (1) Elect the first black President, and (2) Change Politics Forever.

"Please grab a seat or find a spot on the floor," Ford directed the crowd. "I'm going to get started." Gianna scurried for a seat next to Ford and gazed upon him with admiration. The others quickly grabbed seats as well and looked eagerly at him. He bowed his head and raised his arms, like a band conductor, quieting one half of the room with his left hand, and then indicating with his right hand to follow the other half's lead. Once everyone was quiet, he raised his head and began.

"All of you should either be settled in your supporter housing or be prepared to head there directly after the meeting." Lily double-checked her notes for Elizabeth Morrow's address. Should she bring a bottle of wine? A pie?

"If you are unsure of your housing assignment, please see Gianna. She has worked very hard to set all of this up for you. It is critical to the success of our campaign that you live with your supporter in the community in which you are working. You all have been strategically assigned turf based on my determination." He surveyed the crowed. "For those of you who are wondering whether your turf has been racially assigned, it has."

Most of the staffers were black or white. She spotted two Asians on staff.

"You two," Ford seemed momentarily confused at the thought. "You're on the white turf.

"The first thing that you will be doing once you are in your turf is to locate an office. You will work with your RFD on this project. You should lean on the volunteers that have been identified in the My Campaign database during the primary. Rachel, our Voter File Manager, will go over this with you; she has created an activist code for volunteers likely to help find an in-kinded office."

The last list of volunteers she had for a campaign was on an excel sheet on a Gateway desktop.

Parker leaned toward her, "I'll translate later."

"You heard me correctly: you must find offices that are in-kinded."

Sam whispered to Lily, "Donated."

"Gianna is currently heading up operations while we wait for an Ops Director from Denver; she will walk you through the paperwork required once the office is located. Gianna will be your RFD's point of contact for all resource issues. You do not call Gianna directly; you call your RFD and he calls Gianna. This is how the chain of communication works and it is essential that you follow it. You have one goal right now: to register voters. To get to that goal you will need to recruit and activate volunteers. Some of you in predominantly white turf will begin the persuasion phase on an earlier time line."

"That's us," Parker informed her.

"Persuasion involves exactly what the term means. Persuading independents and the Ryan Democrats on the issues to vote for Cady. Please work in MyCampaign. This is Rachel. She is going to introduce you to Georgia and give you training on the van. You have three weapons in this battle: the van, your laptop, and your cell phone. Period."

"Hello everyone, I'm Rachel, your data diva. For anyone who doesn't know, the VAN is not a VW minibus, but the Voter Activation Network. It has all the voting data for the state."

Ah. Lily knew she liked Rachel immediately.

"But, before you get started, I want to let you know why it is so important that you have chosen to come to Georgia to work for Cady. There are over 600,000 unregistered eligible African Americans in this state. That's a lot of people who you can directly impact and bring into the process!"

There were some "yeahs" in the room, but mostly people reviewed their folders. The unregistered numbers was daunting. Lily had voted since she was 18, but had never had to convince anyone else to register, let alone vote.

"The work that you do will build a legacy in this state. This is amazing! No campaign has ever reached the four corners of this state like ours will. We will build neighborhood organizing teams that will hopefully exist long after we are gone. This is real organizing on such a fundamental level. I cannot believe that I get to be a part of this. If you do this right, you will make history and change the electorate forever ... not to mention get Cady elected."

This time the same "yeahs" yeahed louder. There was some rustling in the room. A few coughs. A couple of people left to use the bathroom. She admired Rachel's enthusiasm and her own excitement began to grow.

"Now, here is information about how to build community teams. If you turn to page 5 ..." Page 5 was projected onto the screen. It was titled "Community Organizing Fundamentals."

"Rachel." Ford interrupted. "I'm sorry to stop you but I have Davis Wright, himself, on the phone. He wants to talk to Georgia." She heard gasps across room.

"Georgia. This is Davis Wright calling from Denver." The room cheered.

"I cannot express to you enough how excited we are about what you are about to do in Georgia. This is a unique moment in time and a unique candidate who is so appealing that we can actually run a campaign in Georgia."

His voice was abrupt, quick, and surprisingly, slightly squeaky. When she'd seen him on Meet the Press just a couple of weeks ago, he looked like he had just stepped away from a beer pong game, rather than suited up to spearhead a Presidential campaign.

"Who would've guessed 8 years ago when we were fucked in Florida or 4 years ago when we were just fucked that you would be standing in Georgia listening to *ME* on the phone. Fantastic. Georgia is the new Ohio. Go kick some ass!"

The room erupted. Two staffers behind Lily hugged her. A bright-eyed staffer in clean, white sneakers and a neatly ironed oxford whose name tag read, "Tim Washington, RFD, City of Atlanta," grabbed her shoulders. "The new Ohio! When we win Georgia, I'm going straight to D.C. The DOJ!" Although he was tall and thin, his hands felt strong around her. His swarthy bald head shined beneath the lights and his wide smile sparkled with confidence, which reminded her of a younger version of Cady.

A woman from behind them chimed in, "I'm following my girl Valerie wherever she goes!" Valerie Campbell had launched her own modest bid for the Presidency that quickly came to an end even before the Iowa caucus, yet she had garnered fiercely loyal supporters in that time. Lily hadn't met one in person until now. The woman's dark coarse hair was cut short and braided tightly against her head. Her glasses, which rested securely around her ears, couldn't hide the fierceness in her eyes. She wore a tank top, which reflected her slim build and well-defined muscles that seemed alert and ready to strike on moment's notice. Her nametag read, "Angela Lake, City of Atlanta." Tim scowled at Angela's remark and she lunged toward him in response. He recoiled.

"Where do you want to work?" Tim asked Lily.

She shrugged. "I don't know." She hadn't thought about what was next after the campaign. For the first time she wasn't planning ahead. She was ready to channel surf life for a while. And for the moment, she had stopped in Georgia.

Ford dismissed the crowd, "Let's go change the world. Let's go kick some ass." She pulled out her Georgia road map so she could find the asses she was supposed to kick.

CHAPTER 6

Atlanta's congested interstates soon seemed as distant as New York as Lily wended her way through the state and local highways of rural Georgia. The landscape turned to red clay and brown fields, and gun shops, barbecue joints, bail bonds and pawnshops, tractor vendors, a density of fast food restaurants, and the ubiquitous discount shopping store SaveAlot — the icon that united any contemporary small-town-dotted stretches of farmland. This was no Greenwich Village. This must be the OTP Jerry mentioned. She had yet to spot a Chinese restaurant. Finally, in what she was pretty sure was Ludlow, she stumbled onto a relic of a town square where the storefronts were boarded, except for a hardware store, Bethlehem Lock and Key, and a bakery/café named Latte Da. A waiter leaned against the glass door to the entrance of the café, a cigarette in one hand and a tennis ball in the other. He bounced the ball against the lamppost. From the storefront windows she couldn't see a single patron inside the café.

"Excuse me." She rolled down the passenger door window. "Where is Sugarplum Road?"

He hesitated, narrowing his eyes and furrowing his brow, as if unsure whether to trust her with directions. "Keep straight down here, until you gotta make a decision. Then go left."

"Is there a landmark? Street name?" He bounced the ball quicker and closer. Hitting the trashcan beside her car.

"Go left when you need to decide," he repeated. The ball now rested in his hands. He circled it between two fingers, as if deciding what to hit next.

She drove quickly past the café. She passed another fast food chain, a dollar store, and a water tower, until she arrived at a T-Junction. This must be it. It was time to turn left. The road was sprinkled with one-story ranch houses amidst magnolia trees in spectacular white bloom. Gated fences were wrapped with honeysuckle. She found Elizabeth Morrow's house at the end of the street. She had never heard of supporter housing before. Elizabeth must be extremely nice or extremely crazy to house someone for free for 5 months. The house was one of the few in the neighborhood with a Cady yard sign. Weirdly though, none was actually posted in the yard. One hung high between the branches on the tree, another inside a window, and one was propped up on the roof of a house. The Morrows had their sign affixed to the top of the garage.

She parked her car behind a white pick-up truck that took nearly three quarters of the driveway. A man, sporting a baseball cap over dirty blond hair, ambled over to her. Both his t-shirt and blue jeans were streaked with oil and grass stains. He appeared too young to be Mr. Morrow. She double checked the address and her notes. Elizabeth Morrow, Age 67.

"I guess I'll have to replant those flower beds," he commented has he stood by her car.

Lily looked behind her and saw tire tracks over crushed begonias along the side of the driveway.

"Oh, I'm so sorry. I'll help you." These nice people had opened up their home to her and she'd already begun to destroy it.

"When's the last time you planted something?" He joked.

"You're right. I somehow managed to kill my indoor cactus, by not watering it enough."

His smile exposed a few wrinkles around his eyes and mouth, but his grey blue eyes shined a brighter blue.

"You must be Lily. I'm Luke. Elizabeth's son." His hand was rough with calluses and cuts.

"Yes, that's me." He opened the front door for Lily and carried her things into the house. The last time anyone carried her things was when she sprained her ankle, and even then she tipped the doorman nicely for the trouble.

"Nice car. German?"

"Swedish."

"Not a lot of those around here." Damn it, Gabe was right.

Once inside, she relaxed. She heard the popping of oil the minute she entered the house. She could smell the crispy skin of chicken. The house was dated, containing furniture that could only be moved by four strong men, but it was uncluttered and the deep couch was inviting. Framed black and white photos decorated the fireplace mantle. An old box television and a radio tuner sat on a corner shelf. Luke showed her the guest bedroom, which contained a four-post white frame bed and a quilt draped on its edge. She felt like slumbering and awaking three months later.

"Lily, is that you?" Elizabeth called from the kitchen. "I hope the house wasn't too difficult to find." She wore baggy white pants and a bright blue tunic. Her silvery gray hair was swept loosely off her neck, so that a few strands framed her face. Her reading glasses hung on a strap around her neck, giving her the look of a college professor.

"Not at all."

"Welcome to our home. Please make yourself comfortable. We are very excited to have you in our home as you work on the Cady campaign," she beamed. She darted a glance at Luke.

"Yeah. Sure." His warm welcome had disappeared and Lily wondered why. Was he that upset about the begonias?

"I hope you're hungry. There's plenty of food." Elizabeth began to set the table. As a guest, she couldn't refuse dinner. She would run an extra lap around the neighborhood tomorrow morning.

"Thanks, mom, but I've got other plans." He kissed Elizabeth on the cheek, gave Lily a nod, and left the house. Lily felt a tinge of disappointment, but then relief. She wouldn't want to be distracted by blue grey eyes her first night on the Campaign.

She pulled out the wine she had picked up from a supermarket off the highway.

"Pinot?" she asked. They settled into a dinner of fried chicken, mashed potatoes, and collard greens. Until now, she'd only paired fried chicken with the tangy cheese sauce and a biscuit. The wine blended perfectly. She could grow quite comfortable here.

"So Lily, why did you decide to come here?" Elizabeth asked as she served another heaping scoop of mashed potatoes.

"I actually didn't choose. I was assigned to Georgia."

"Oh." A flash of disappointment crossed Elizabeth's face.

But Lily quickly recovered. "I'm glad I'm here, though. It's a historic place and quite beautiful." She recalled the long stretches of farmland in between Atlanta and Ludlow, and pushed the bail bonds shops and SaveAlot out of her mind.

"Well, I was a latecomer to the south myself." Elizabeth smiled. "I grew up in Michigan, but fell in love with a redneck from Georgia. Charles recently passed away, so Luke moved into the garage apartment to help out."

Lily instinctively laid her hand on Elizabeth's. A hand that despite the wrinkles felt strong. "I'm sorry."

"Oh, it was such an adventure. I wouldn't have wanted anything else." Her eyes twinkled more blue than grey, just like Luke's.

"How's it going so far? I'm thrilled that the campaign is here. You know, I lived in supporter housing myself nearly 40 years ago, when I traveled during the movement. It's how I met Charles."

"Oh, I haven't been working on the campaign long. So I haven't really met anyone." Nor did she think she would. The campaign workers were cute and enthusiastic, but not one seemed like a romantic possibility, despite the age difference of a few years.

"I didn't think I would either." Elizabeth smiled sheepishly.

"Well, the first thing I have to do is locate an office space. A very cheap office space. Really, a free one."

"Luke can help you with that tomorrow. I'll ask him to show you around."

"Oh, no. That's ok. I can figure it out."

"It's not a bother at all."

Dessert was warm pecan pie with homemade vanilla ice cream. Lily could make camp beside the kitchen table forever. Elizabeth then turned on the radio to a local jazz station. The old radio tuner and its oversized speakers filled the whole house with music. The trumpet soared and the electric guitar provided the rhythm to which they washed dishes. No dishwasher; only a dish rack. Elizabeth retired into the main room to watch the late evening news, and Lily excused herself early to call Gabe and her parents. She was actually thankful she reached their voicemails. She wanted to savor her first night in Ludlow without their voices in her head. And while the morning had been disorienting, she felt settled in Elizabeth's home. She snuggled into bed and picked up the book Rachel had given her. She was soon immersed in Lovell's account of the midnight drives he and his fellow colleagues made in the '60s through the rural parts of Georgia and Alabama, avoiding trouble with local law enforcement or hostile groups, while searching for a bathroom that the women could use. Ford's late night call interrupted her absorption.

"Have you secured office space, yet?"

"I just got here a couple of hours ago."

"Lily, we need that space asap."

"It's 10 o'clock at night. I'll do it first thing tomorrow," and he hung up.

Her comfort quickly gave way to irritation. She wanted to find a space. But without a budget how could she? She drifted in and out of sleep, worried about the next day. The slam of the garage apartment door woke her around 1 a.m. She hoped Luke didn't mind helping. She finally drifted off at 3 a.m.

They set off in his truck early the next morning. Luke's silence suggested he either needed another cup of coffee or was annoyed that his mother forced him to do this. At this point, she didn't care. She needed another coffee too. And if Elizabeth had tied Luke's arms together and thrown him into the back of the pick-up, she would've taken it. She settled into the seat and leaned her head against the open window frame as the landscape turned from ranch homes to farmland to the center of town through which she passed the day before. Latte Da had opened for breakfast, but still no one was inside. They took a roundabout out of the square into a four way stop intersected by railroad tracks filled with overgrown bushes and thickets of wildflowers unhampered by any train. Northeast of the intersection was a street lined with beautiful antebellum houses. She spotted the Republican Party flag flying above one of the homes. Dale Eaves signs sprinkled the yard. A red, white, and blue banner announced proudly the site of Eaves's local campaign office. The road to the southwest was dotted with Soviet-style housing complexes and a trailer park. "The other side of the tracks" was clearly not a literary device. They crossed over.

She finally broke the silence. "Thanks for driving me around this morning. I hope you didn't miss work or anything."

"Sure," he replied; his eyes still focused on the road ahead. He wore the same clothes as the night before.

"So Elizabeth said you recently moved in. Where did you live before?"

"Chicago."

"Really? What did you do there?"

"Worked."

She wanted to pry, but didn't have the time. She needed an office and it could take an entire two days worth of driving in silence before he would reveal anything. They pulled up to a tiny house, not much bigger than her parents' garage. But it had a porch swing with a little old lady wearing a pink and white striped hat sipping iced tea. She looked so relaxed it made Lily want to switch places with her for just one moment.

"Hello Lucas!" the lady called out from the swing as they pulled into the driveway.

"Can I call you that?" Lily asked.

"She's the only one who calls me that. Hi there, Miss Louise," Luke replied and kissed the woman on her rosy brown cheek as fondly as he did his own mother.

"Now, who is this young lady?" Although she smiled when she asked, her voice sharpened and her eyebrows arched.

"This is Lily. She works on Ramal Cady's campaign."

Miss Louise jumped out of the swing, spilling her iced tea. Luke quickly mopped up the spill with a rag he carried in his back pocket.

"Wonderful. So wonderful! I feel so honored that you are here in Ludlow." Her eyes widened and her smile reached nearly from ear to ear. Lily couldn't help but give her a hug.

"Lily is in charge of securing an office location, and I thought you're the perfect person for her to chat with."

"Oh, my. Is this for the campaign?" she exclaimed. Lily nodded. "Well, I have the perfect location right near the center of town," Miss Louise offered. Lily recalled the charming homes she had seen and grew excited. Perhaps it was that vacant Victorian next to the flower shop? Or, if it was right next door to Eaves's office she would outfit it with spy cameras. She salivated at the idea of her own campaign war room.

"I have an old place where I used to print my t-shirts."

"That will work," Lily replied instantly. She didn't have any other options. The front porch would work.

"Oh, wonderful. Let us meet there tomorrow at 9:00 a.m. Lucas knows where it is."

"Thank you so much, Miss Louise."

"Anything for Cady, Lily. Anything."

As they drove away, Luke explained how to draw up a contract with Miss Louise.

"So the rent should only be about $400 a month—"

"I thought the space was free."

"Free? What do you mean?"

She found herself explaining rather sheepishly, "We don't really have a budget. All of our offices need to be in-kinded, which means donated."

"Donated? Since when are office spaces donated?"

"Don't most campaigns operate that way?"

"Maybe by wealthy supporters. But you're asking *Miss Louise* to fund the campaign's operations?"

"I guess we pick up the utilities and such." Ford never explained the details.

"You guess? What about supplies, equipment, computers, and internet?" He rattled off all the things that were lurking in the back of her mind. The things she was afraid to ask Ford about.

"I don't know. Yet."

"You don't know?"

"You sound like a lawyer." He quickly grew quiet. "Are you one?"

"No. I just fix things."

"It's only my second day. I'll figure it out. But you saw how happy she was to help the campaign. She basically would do "anything" for Cady. I think she'd be fine with donating the space. Most people are that excited just to be involved with the campaign." She parroted Ford's advice with restrained conviction.

"Well, not most."

"Right. Definitely not you."

"Cady already has a 20 million dollar campaign chest and you're asking someone who lives paycheck to paycheck to donate."

She wouldn't be able to convince him of the campaign's position any time soon. For once, she was happy to be interrupted by Ford's call.

"Did you secure an office space?"

Lily could feel Luke's stare. "Yes. I do have a question about reimbursements …"

"Great. I've notified the local media that there will be an official office opening tomorrow. Expect press there around 11. Email me the address. Sam and Parker will make phone calls tonight to all those who signed up on Cady's volunteer portion of the campaign website. Expect 30 volunteers. That's your region's goal."

"Wait, I haven't even seen it yet. I don't know if it's media ready."

"Things move fast here. Read your handbook." He hung up.

She heaved a sigh and asked Luke, "So are you willing to tell me the address to the place?" To her relief, Luke nodded.

CHAPTER 7

She wrestled through another sleepless night. What if no one showed up to the office opening, except the reporter? Then again, what if people did show up? What exactly would she say to them? What would the reporter say she said? And why the hell was she notified at the last minute about the opening? Was Ford sabotaging her? Everything seemed last minute. What would she tell Miss Louise about rent and utilities? She didn't have an answer for that. What did the office space even look like? She watched the clock tick away — 2:30 a.m..

She was exhausted from riding in the car all day. After Luke had dropped her home, she spent the rest of the afternoon driving around Ludlow and getting lost on the country highways. In New York, she identified North, South, East, and West based on which side the Empire State Building came into view. Here the landmarks all looked alike — a gas station on one side of the street with an empty building with a "For Lease" sign across from it. There was a "For Lease" sign every mile. After a few miles down Highway 17, she had discovered SaveAlot's complex. Cars waited patiently to enter the sprawling compound. She got in line.

Once inside, she saw more than triple the number of people than the number of houses on her drive from Atlanta to Ludlow. Mothers shopped for the week's groceries, while fathers played with the children in the SaveAlot playground, doling quarters into the mechanical pigs, unicorns, and horses for their kids to ride. She overheard two ladies discuss the jeans' sizes in Spanish. In the international foods aisle, there was kimchi, gyoza, berbere, and curry. SaveAlot was the intersection of all ages, races, and accents in a 20-mile radius of Ludlow, akin to a subway ride in New York. She purchased an oversized Cady t-shirt and khaki shorts. They now lay on the bedroom dresser. 2:34 a.m. She called Gabe.

"Still awake?"

"I am now. What's up? I've got to get up at the crack of dawn. Crop rotation."

"Everything is completely disorganized and last minute. I can't work like that."

"Yes, you can."

"I can't. The press is coming. I haven't even seen the office. Who knows if anyone will show?"

"Do you have snacks? People show up for snacks."

"Snacks is your answer?"

"Yes. Snacks is my final answer."

She laughed. "Good night. Love ya."

"Love ya more."

She forced herself to get some sleep. She would return to SaveAlot early in the morning for snacks.

When she arrived at the space the next morning, she realized all her fears had come true. This place made the Atlanta Headquarters look like the Waldorf. The vinyl siding building lay ten feet from the railroad tracks in an empty gravel lot. Across the street was a Shell gas station and a liquor store, behind it a housing project. Holes in the windows were patched with cardboard and duct tape. Sure, this was in the central part of town, just on the other side of town from the Victorian mansions.

"Oh, Lillian, welcome!" Lily hid her disappointment. It was difficult to sour in front of Miss Louise. "Come inside. Let me give you the tour."

As they strolled across the torn carpet, Miss Louise beamed at the thought of turning this "old space that hasn't been used in who knows how many years into a campaign headquarters." Rattraps lay in corners, and dead bugs flopped beside them. There was no air conditioner. It was almost June and she felt faint in the sweltering heat. She had toyed with the idea of the Peace Corps in college. Not anymore.

Miss Louise hesitated at the only closet in the room.

"This is where we keep the shotgun."

"Shotgun?"

"Just in case." Lily searched her face for a hint of humor and found none. She was serious. Miss Louise opened the closet door. It looked like the kind of shotgun that she'd seen on television. Brown handle with a long black nose. It hung from a hook, the barrel of the gun dangling from its strap. A box of shells lay beneath it on a shelf. Not only had Lily never fired a gun, she had never worked in the same room as one. She gently grazed her fingers against the brown handle, like she would a kitten. Her finger circled the trigger. "I'll show you how to load and fire it, just in case." Miss Louise closed the closet door, just as the front door squeaked open. An old man wearing torn jeans and a flannel shirt stumbled in.

"Larry, the liquor store is across the street," Miss Louise reminded him.

He removed his hat and bowed his head. "Sorry, ma'am." He stumbled out.

"Excuse me Miss Louise. I need to make a call." She followed Larry to the liquor store.

"Ford, this isn't going to work. I need time to find something else." How was she going to turn what was essentially an extra-large shed into a campaign headquarters without any freaking money? The place needed to be razed and built anew.

"Sorry, Lily. There is no time. Reporter will be there in 2 hours."

"Ford, I'm serious." She followed Larry inside.

"I'm serious too. It's free and that's all that matters."

"Well, where are Sam and Parker? They were supposed to help."

"Oh, they got caught up, but they'll be there soon." She yearned to reach across the cellular network and strangle him by his bowtie. She bought a bottle of whiskey and returned to the shed.

"It's a slippery slope. Drinking on the job," said Miss Louise. She glanced at her watch. "Especially at 9 a.m."

"I'm already sliding, Miss Louise." She took a quick swig of the bottle. She coughed it up, as the whiskey burned in the back of her throat.

"Dear, why don't you hand me that bottle? I'll take care of it while you start thinking about your next step?" Miss Louise took the bottle and put it on a shelf. She couldn't flush it down the toilet, because it didn't work! She needed to pull herself together and figure out a way to turn this space into an operable office in less than two hours. The same way as a lawyer she had constructed a financing agreement in less than one hour. She switched to frantic mode.

"Miss Louise, I need a gallon of bleach and a pile of rags." Miss Louise unearthed a pile of discarded t-shirts and a gallon of Lysol from the closet. The two of them began to work very quickly. Lily aimed for halfway decent, which meant a quick wipedown of the walls and furniture and spraying the corners with a pine scented air-guard. She also called on Luke to fix the broken toilet. He did so without protest. Sam and Parker arrived just in time to help make poster board signs to indicate that this was Cady's campaign office. Now she understood the Atlanta office's condition.

"Hungry?" asked Parker. She handed Lily a white paper bag with Chick N' Bik printed in red. Lily dropped the trash bag she was holding.

"Where in the world did you get this?"

"Off Highway 18."

"I love those chicken biscuits with that tangy cheese sauce, not sure what it's called…"

"Pimento cheese," said Parker.

"What?"

"It's made from pimento cheese. Chick N' Bik is based in Georgia."

Immediately, Lily's nerves settled. The whiskey could wait. She quickly ate her two biscuits and silently thanked Parker for the normal portion size.

"We called about forty people last night and asked them to show up to today's office opening," said Sam.

"There are forty Cady supporters around here?" Lily asked as she wiped the cheese sauce off her face. She wanted more.

"In a twenty mile radius," Sam admitted. "But they did sign up on line to volunteer."

"That's good. We should meet our goal of thirty then, right?" asked Lily.

"Hopefully," muttered Parker.

"What about supplies?" Sam asked. "You know, paper, phone lines, internet access."

"You can't get high speed internet out here." Miss Louise explained. "Only dial-up."

This must be worse than the Peace Corps. Didn't Bill Gates singlehandedly wire all of Africa? Maybe he should put rural Georgia on his list. She called Ford for answers.

"Get what you can. You'll have to make do with dial-up until we can figure it out, but in the meantime see if the volunteers can donate."

"Why don't we take a break and go down to SaveAlot?" Parker suggested as she sidled up to Sam and bumped up against his arm. He kissed her on her forehead, then on her nose, followed by the cheeks, chin, and finally the mouth.

"No. We don't have any money," Lily replied shortly.

"We're going to search my Jeep to see if there's anything we can use." Sam winked at Parker as the two of them sneaked out.

Lily was already nervous about making a speech and now she had to ask for donations. Luke cast her yet another disapproving glance. She let it pass. There was no time to argue.

By the time 11 a.m. approached, her anxiety had peaked. The high from the tangy pimento cheese sauce had worn off. She paced the office hoping that somebody showed up. With Luke gone, Miss Louise running errands, and Sam and Parker endlessly gazing at each other, Lily felt alone in this endeavor. Alone in Ludlow. As the clock ticked past 11, for the second time that day her fears were realized. The reporter from the Barrow County News appeared to an empty room. She ushered Sam and Parker, who had since emerged from Sam's truck with tousled hair and flushed faces, into the seats to boost the audience quotient from zero to two. "Pretend you guys are volunteers," she instructed.

"Welcome." She greeted the reporter forcefully and louder than needed. It was becoming a nervous habit for her to speak like a car salesman. He smiled meekly in return and took a seat in the back. He began to take notes, rather copiously for an event that hadn't even occurred. If he had only seen what the window looked like before the new duct tape patchwork. Elizabeth arrived next, waved hello, sat next to the reporter, and peeked at his notes. Ford had assured her that an email had been sent to all local Cady supporters alerting them of the Ludlow office opening and campaign-kickoff. What if they didn't open the message? After a couple of very long minutes, minutes where Lily contemplated feigning an illness or proclaiming mission accomplished, a skinny teenager with shaggy hair and wire glasses slumped in, wearing shorts and a baggy black t-shirt imprinted with a skull labeled "Tarranon." He was followed by a slim, beautiful woman with honey-brown skin, wearing a tailored suit and carrying a Chanel bag. She took the middle seat in the front row and was undeterred by the spider that quickly made its way up her bag. She swiftly killed it with a rolled-up newspaper, and dumped paper and corpse in the trash. Finally, a middle-aged couple rushed in wearing University of Georgia Bulldog football t-shirts and shorts. She was in red with black lettering. He was in white with red and black lettering. They apologized for their tardiness. Moments later Miss Louise returned.

Six people, Sam and Parker, and a reporter. She stood before their eager faces wondering where to begin. This was her crew, her Kitchen Cabinet, her battalion, with which she had to win Northeast Georgia. Oh boy. Cady had said this was a "bottom up" campaign. Well, she certainly was at the bottom. She could forget any vacation time between now and November.

After a brief introduction, and as instructed by the Organizer Training handbook, she asked each volunteer to tell his or her story of why they support the campaign.

"I lost my health insurance last year," said Sarah of the couple, Sarah and Ken, who rushed in late. "I've got some health problems and can't get insurance now." Others nodded in empathy.

The beautiful woman stood up and turned to address the room from her front chair. "I'm Denise from Philadelphia. I'm new here to Georgia. I've always been a Democrat and always will be." She eyed everyone intently. "But I learned after the last two elections. It's not enough just to vote any more." Everyone echoed her with yeses. *Not enough just to vote.* Good motivation line. Lily jotted it down in her notebook for future reference.

James, the disheveled teenager explained from his seat, "Cady is different. He seems to actually want the job." Very insightful, she thought. Yes, it was true. Cady appeared more interested in the challenges of the job than in simply winning.

Miss Louise stood up next. "I've lived in Georgia my whole life. My father and his father too. And I sometimes don't believe all of this is real. That Cady could actually be President. Like this is some dream and somebody will wake me soon enough. But y'all being here. It's making it feel more real. You all feel real. And I'm just so ..." Her voice trailed off and she paused to gather herself. Elizabeth stood up next to her and touched her shoulder. "I'm so pleased."

"I agree," said Elizabeth. "I've been in Ludlow for 40 years now. It's a beautiful town. I do love it. But it's a small town. And, well after Charles passed away, I've been laying low. I'm ready to shake things up again." The others shouted in agreement. "Lily, tell us how to shake things up."

Lily laid out her strategy, which was comprised of words parroted from Davis Wright.

"I want to explain how we can win Georgia." She paused for effect. "Georgia is the next Ohio!" The group stared at her with skepticism. The reporter quickly scribbled in his notebook. "Or the next Florida." They remained unconvinced. She thought back to what Rachel said. "Ok. What's important to know is that there are 600,000 unregistered African Americans in this state and we need to register them." Their eyes lit up at the challenge. They nodded in response. "While in this rural part of Georgia we may be the underdog, we just have to do our part. And, across the state volunteers just like you will do their part." The group looked eager, ready to work. "And, if everyone does their part, we will win Georgia!" The small but mighty group clapped, with Denise leading a standing ovation. Even the reporter appeared excited. Sam and Parker cheered for her as well.

"I'm ready to get to work!" chimed Sarah. Ken and the other agreed. Lily rattled off the supplies they needed and Denise offered to go buy them. Sarah and Ken volunteered to scout out the areas where they could find registrations. James went to the local library that had high-speed internet access to download call lists from the VAN and then printed them at his high school computer lounge. Lily, Sam, and Parker called the 34 volunteers who hadn't shown up to see if they could attend the next meeting. Elizabeth and Miss Louise finished cleaning the nooks and crannies of the office, and Luke reinforced its loose screws.

By 9:30 p.m. that night, Lily locked up the office, waved goodbye to Sam and Parker as they made the hour drive back to their apartment in Buckhead, and basked in the volunteers' achievement today. She dialed into the regional field directors' nightly conference call with Ford and proudly described the commitment of her small group.

"The goal was thirty volunteers," Ford interrupted.

"Yes, but their effort was like thirty."

"We'll talk about this later. Ok, let's move on to Middle Georgia. Tell us about your event. How many volunteers?"

She arrived back home a deflated. Nothing pleased Ford. Elizabeth had left out a bottle of wine and a glass for her with a note "A toast on your first day."

CHAPTER 8

Elizabeth woke Lily up early the next morning with a cup of coffee and the Barrow County news. "You're — I mean we're — in the paper!" This was the first time Lily had been in any paper, except for her college paper when her building had been condemned for asbestos. Now she was in one that might actually pay for its articles.

"Do you know I've never been in the papers? Never during the '60s. I wasn't on the front lines. I just provided logistical support in the background. I guess I hadn't done anything newsworthy after that. Just taught high school for 30 years, but, this is … this is simply wonderful." Elizabeth paused, realizing she was still in Lily's bedroom doorway. "I'll let you read in privacy."

She left Lily alone with the coffee. It wasn't like reading the New York Times. The paper had 8 pages typed in 18-sized font. But she appreciated the coffee in bed. She flipped past stories about the upcoming high school football season and the latest church fundraiser, and found a picture of the Ludlow office tucked in between the obituaries and the wedding announcements. The reporter gave a semi-favorable review of their effort: "A small group of Cady devotees gathered in a cottage on the south side of town yesterday to accomplish the daunting task of campaigning in the Northeast region of the state for Ramal Cady, the Democratic Presidential nominee, a region in which the Republican candidate for President in the previous election won with 75% of the votes. In spite of the odds, this small group appeared motivated."

Lily felt lightly heartened by the report's description of the office as a cottage. 75 percent Republican? No wonder they put a newbie out here in the hinterlands. No wonder Sam and Parker grimaced at the thought. She looked over the goals that Ford provided. Registration: 20,000 people. Persuasion: 40,000. Vote Goal: 60,000. That was 60,000 more Democrats than in the previous Presidential election. Sure, Cady wasn't going to "win" this region. But her goal was to increase the Democratic votes by an additional 7% to 32% from the previous 25% of the last election.

The smell of maple syrup wafted through the room. Elizabeth was making her a celebratory breakfast. She had made two so far that week, including the one when she moved in. But any lingering excitement from the success of the day before had evaporated. She reread the news article. How on earth would six people meet this impossible goal? They had no chance.

She struggled through breakfast with a smile, not wanting to dampen Elizabeth's mood. Better to let at least one person feel hopeful.

She needed to find more volunteers. But how? She called Rachel, as she usually found her advice helpful.

"You need to find more people," Rachel instructed.

"Yes, but how?"

"Give it time. They will come."

"That's not a how. I need some specific, practical steps."

"They first have to trust you."

She continued her search for answers on the car drive to the office. In just a week she could drive, sip coffee, and chat via speakerphone all at once. The phone lay in her lap.

"Paying people would be much easier," Gabe remarked. He was laying irrigation pipes in New Jersey as she drove by farmland in Georgia.

"There is no money."

"How is that possible?"

"You sound like Luke."

"He sounds like a guy I'd like to meet."

"I don't think you're his type. I actually don't know who would be. He's sort of rough around the edges. A bit laconic."

"Sounds dreamy."

"I'm at the office. Need to run."

"Oh. By the way, there is a spare tire in the trunk in case your wheels pop in that gravel lot of yours."

As soon as she had hung up with Gabe, her dad called. She had missed his call three times already and couldn't avoid it any longer. He would notify the state patrol if she didn't pick up.

"Hey, Dad. Sorry, I've missed you. Things are great. Just really busy."

"Lil, I'm mailing you a new road map of Georgia. I've marked where all the gas stations are on the country highways."

"Ok."

"Also, I'm shipping you a bird-lamp your mother got for your office desk."

"What kind of bird? I can handle a canary or a dove, but not a rooster."

He laughed in response. "It's actually a bald eagle. She thought it would inspire you."

"Where on earth—"

"The Central Jersey swap meet."

"I'll take it."

She returned to her desk and found a red magic marker in a coffee canister. She wrote out the goals on poster-sized paper and tacked it on the wall in the center of the room, so that no one could miss it. She stared at the large, looming, red numbers for twenty minutes letting the enormous undertaking sink in. Then she began to map out a plan where they could at least make a dent in the registration goal. They could register voters at public parks and festivals. Perhaps the Latte Da café had a busy hour that she wasn't aware of?

"We need to go to the belly of the beast. SaveAlot," Denise declared. She had dropped by the office that morning with more needed supplies. Pens, paper, printer ink. As she busily unpacked and arranged the office, the only thing Lily could think of at the moment was *thank god God for rich, beautiful liberal women.*

"SaveAlot? It's private property. I think we may need to get permission."

"Everyone in a 30 mile radius shops there. It's the only store in town where you can buy your diapers, groceries, and guns."

"Did you know you can get your hair and nails done there too?" She had spotted the indoor salon, but stopped short at reviewing their menu of services. She wasn't ready for full assimilation to contemporary rural life.

Denise was shocked by the thought. She must make the hour and a half trip into Atlanta to fulfill her beauty needs.

"Let me check with Ford and see whether anyone in the campaign has been able to register voters outside of SaveAlot. Maybe they've gotten clearance."

"It really is the only way. Otherwise it would take us months, years to find all those people." Denise surveyed the room. "Much better, don't you think?"

The folding chairs now sported beige fabric covers and purple pillows. Vases filled with daisies and tulips were placed at the volunteer tables. Papers and pens lay in neat organized piles and holders.

"Even better than the Atlanta office." Denise beamed at the compliment. She hoped the forthcoming bald eagle lamp wouldn't clash with the decor.

Ford encouraged them to register at SaveAlot.

"Don't we need permission?"

"Let's see what we can get away with."

"And then ask for forgiveness later? I don't know."

"Lily, we tried to get permission at SaveAlots all across the county. And they denied our requests. Better to let your volunteers just try without." She didn't know how to implement guerrilla tactics, only rules and regulations. She had never once run up a down escalator. She spent the next day embroiled in a SaveAlot bureaucratic nightmare. First she tried the local manager, who sent her to the regional manager, who put her on hold for twenty minutes until she said it was the local manager's decision. But, the local manager feared he would be suspended by the regional manager if he allowed it. Next she called the national office, which mistakenly transferred her to an international office whose operator didn't understand U.S. voting registration requirements or the election, but told her he was rooting for Cady. She called back the national office, which then put her on hold for another twenty minutes and eventually transferred her back to the regional office. She reviewed her Georgia voter registration guidelines, which required them to register only in public spaces. That would mean that to reach anyone at SaveAlot they would have to stand across the parking lot on the other side of the highway. Maybe Ford was right. They should just try to register until they can't. What's the worst they can do? Tell them no.

She worked late into the evening. She hadn't heard a peep from Sam or Parker all day and the office was eerily quiet, except for Larry who had once again mistaken the office for the liquor store.

"Lily?"

After the day she had had with SaveAlot employees, it was nice to hear Luke's voice on the phone. She thought they had grown to like each other over the last couple of days, and maybe they could get past any his lukewarm attitude toward her using Miss Louise's t-shirt making studio as a campaign office. After all, they were living in the same house for the next five months.

"Hi Luke. What's up?"

"I just got a call from my mom. She, along with Denise and the rest of the volunteers, have been arrested. Can you meet me at the jail?"

CHAPTER 9

Lily didn't know which she feared more: Luke's further disdain of the campaign, or the look on the volunteers' imprisoned faces. What if they'd been beaten by a nightstick? Did the police still carry nightsticks? She had read enough of Lovell's memoir to know what the police in these small towns could do to those who fought for democracy. Should she attempt a southern accent and identify them as "POH-leece""? Should she say "y'all"? She would rescue them, in spite of the humidity, which soaked through her t-shirt even at 9 p.m.

She marched into the cinder block jail next to the pawn shop and bail bondsmen in the vacant strip mall on Highway 29, and demanded their release. The fluorescent overhead lights flickered, circled by a buzzing mosquito. The room was bare, except for the skinny kid dressed in a policeman's uniform who sat behind the desk playing a hand-held gaming device that looked more advanced than the desktop computer. Bookshelves were lined with half-filled liquor bottles, tagged as evidence.

"Hello, I need to speak with your supervisor." He barely looked 18. His brown hair displayed an even part down the middle. His brown police button-down was neatly tucked into his pants. He didn't carry a gun.

"I'm the only one here." His fingers remained on the game controls.

"Can you please release these six people?" She handed him a slip of paper with their names.

The kid shoved the paper into the drawer. "It's 2,500 for all of them." He resumed his game.

"2,500 dollars?"

"That's the fine for trespassing."

"That seems arbitrary."

"350 per person equals 2100 dollars." This time he stopped the game and glanced up at her as if they might actually have a conversation. "The additional $400 are medical costs."

"Medical costs?"

"The tall lady. She kicked the officer. Sharp heels."

Denise. No small town officer could dilute her Philly blood. "It sounds like you pulled out a random number. Why 2,100?"

"Let me show you." He opened the drawer of the desk and held a solar calculator closer to the light.

"I know how to divide," said Lily.

"Yep. 2100 divided by 6 equals 350." He said proudly, as if he had just won the National Science Fair.

"You've said that, but where does it say $350? According to what law?" She suddenly realized she hadn't eaten anything all day. Her throat felt dry and she scouted the room for a water cooler. None. The officer's desk was bare of a candy bowl. The mosquito buzzed closer to her and she started to swat it, missing every time.

"The fine is $2100. There's nothing more to say. Once you pay it, then I'll release them."

"What do you mean you have nothing more to say?" She started to smell her own body odor as the air grew thicker. Where was the fan? He simply stood there, unfazed by the heat.

"Ma'am. If you could please?"

She hated *ma'am*. She couldn't be that much older than he.

"It's as if you guys just make up random rules around here. Can't register voters within 200 feet of SaveAlot. But what you really mean is you can't register our voters." She quickly folded her arms over her campaign t-shirt. "And if you do, you pay $2100."

"We don't have any say in that, ma'am."

"Can't have a campaign office within a 100 yards of a polling place. Can't have a non-profit community center be a polling location, but somehow a Baptist church can be."

"Ma'am, I really don't understand what that has to do with—"

"Must have a photo id to register. What about all those who don't drive?"

"Ma'am, you don't want illegals—"

"Do you really think an illegal person wants to vote?! And stop calling me ma'am!"

He finally put the game device down and stood up.

"Ma'am, or Miss, I really don't like to raise my voice, but you need to listen to me. I'm just -"

"You are squelching Democracy!" And with that she threw the game device against the wall. The mosquito stopped buzzing. The device flickered.

"Now you owe $2,585." They glared at each other. She wanted to stomp on the device and shatter it to pieces.

"We'll figure out a way to pay it." She heard Luke's voice from behind. He laid his hand on her back in comfort, and for a moment she relented. The officer smirked. Her outburst provided him with nighttime drama — a break from his otherwise ordinary day. "Can you take us to everyone?" Luke added.

The six of them were crouched closely together in a circle, like campers at a campfire, and regaled Lily and Luke with their own version of the arrest. Denise reenacted the scene where she kicked the officer. The group passed the shoe around the circle, carefully examining the 4-inch designer heel.

"I haven't been in a jail cell in 40 years. The last time I was with your father, and afterward, the thrill of the experience, well, that's how we had your older brother," Elizabeth said to Luke.

"That's great, I think." His face reddened at his mother's revelation.

"Oh, if he could see me now. He'd be so proud."

"I told that SaveAlot manager exactly on which part of his body he could put his savings sign." Denise laughed. "I don't think a woman has ever spoken that way to him before."

Sarah agreed. "We called our son in California and he just couldn't believe how adventurous we'd become." She squeezed Kent's hand as he gave her an adoring glance. This time she wore the white bulldog shirt and he the red one.

James sat in the corner silent. "James, are you ok?" Lily asked.

He nodded. "Charlotte was shopping with her parents and saw me get handcuffed and put into the squad car. She texted me." He paused. "She's never texted me before. She's never even noticed me before." His usual monotone voice finally had an inflection. James was cool. Kent and Sarah adventurous. Elizabeth energized. And, Denise was able to release her urban spirit. All they needed was a live band and an open bar to complement the celebratory mood.

"Guys, I'm so happy you are all safe. And it sounds like you had a little fun along the way. We've got this little problem of a $2,500 fine, though." She would pay for that damn gaming device. The chattering stopped.

"I can pay for it," volunteered Denise. "It's my fault we're here. I shouldn't have kicked him." She grinned.

"No. We're all in this together," Elizabeth declared. "If you end up paying now, you'll be asked to pay for everything down the road. This is just going to get tougher." Lily shot Elizabeth a *why can't we let generous rich people pay for stuff* look. There was too much to do. Twenty thousand registrations. "We need to solve this problem collectively," Elizabeth continued. The others nodded in agreement.

"We can pay $200," announced Sarah. Kent looked at her with surprise. "I have a separate savings account from you," she whispered.

James explained he had $100 saved from bagging groceries, and the others piped in as well. "This still makes us short $1000." Lily looked over at Luke. He suggested they discuss it outside.

"They were volunteering on behalf of the Presidential candidate. Isn't there a budget for something like this?"

"There isn't a budget for anything," she confessed.

He wasn't too surprised by her answer. As if he knew this all along and was waiting for her finally to admit it. She called Ford for help.

"Just find a new group of volunteers." Only Ford would think free help was replaceable.

"They don't grow on trees out here in Ludlow." He had no response. She decided to call Rachel for advice, and she was thrilled by the predicament.

"Jail time! This is the real deal!"

"Where am I going to find $1,000?"

"This might be the perfect time to outreach to the greater community. The churches and community centers. Let them know what's going on there." Ah yes, the churches. For the cause, for Cady, and for her volunteers she would suck it up and go to church.

"So does anyone know of a good church around here?" She asked the group in the jail cell. Miss Louise perked up.

"That's a great idea! My church. First AME Baptist Church. Just over on Hillside. I think they could help us."

Lily hesitated. "I really wouldn't know what to say." She'd only been to church twice in her life. Once as a child when her mother was experimenting with religion, and again at a church dance during her Bobby Rader crush days.

"I'll go with you." Miss Louise waved to where officer junior sat. "He'll let me out."

"I don't know. He's pretty adamant about the fine."

"He'll let me out for church service," Miss Louise explained. "This will be so wonderful. People will be so excited to hear from you. And afterward you must stay for lunch."

CHAPTER 10

She patted down the ruffles on her dress, but they remained puffy, making her hips appear three sizes larger. The dress, made of taffeta, was Tiffany blue and had been advertised as such. Gabe was right about the unflattering look of such material, particularly in pastels. Only wear dark colors in sheer, smooth materials. She made the most of what SaveAlot had to offer, though. She dared to get her hair trimmed at the salon. As a result, her brown bangs were cut just slightly too short above her eyebrows. On any other day she would've been horrified. This time, she remained poised, like when she won the grade school spelling bee and had to dine with the teachers on the cafeteria stage while the rest of the class sat below.

"You're going to Church in rural Georgia? Don't they speak in tongues and banish unwed mothers to the forest?" Gabe would not recognize her in her new white buckled sandals.

"This is an AME church. Not the Salem witch trials."

"It's like you're in enemy camp. You shop at SaveAlot, you go to Church, and you've stopped drinking. I'm not sure what to make of this." He was right. She hadn't had a drink in at least a couple of days. She was overdue. And since Elizabeth only drank on special occasions, Lily didn't want Elizabeth to find her in bed with a bottle.

"The other night I had a dream that Cady himself was correcting the hand gestures I made during trainings."

"Never point."

"I know."

"Use the thumb."

"I try, but my thumb has a weird shape. Points inward."

"How much weight have you gained, again?"

"I don't know exactly. I haven't gotten on a scale since I left New York." She was afraid. From the stretch of her waistband, she knew it was definitely a few.

"I don't understand."

"Have you ever had fried pickles? They're really tasty."

"You've got to pull yourself together."

"Don't tell me not to eat fried pickles, Gabe. Not today. Not while I'm wearing this Tiffany blue dress."

"Don't call it that. It's the color of the freaking box. Not a dress."

"It's how it was advertised down here. Did I tell you there was a Chick N' Bik just a few miles away?"

"Uh oh."

"They are based in Georgia!"

"Oh, no."

"I know you all think Cady is the perfect candidate, but down here, he's just a black man with a funny sounding name. I saw a rally sign questioning whether he's even American, *because he may have Native American in his blood.* Do you realize what I'm dealing with?! I can't be expected to exercise and eat healthy, also. That's asking too much." She would eat fried chicken at lunch and drink sugar in her iced tea. They called it sweet tea for a reason. Then she would get a prescription for her cholesterol. This was America, after all.

There was dead silence on the line. "Gabe?"

"I'm sending you a care package."

"Don't."

"Liquefied vegan shots. It is what actors and models take when they are on a shoot far off in the jungle."

"Thanks."

She heard the car horn outside. Miss Louise was punctual. "Gotta go, Gabe."

"Bye. And be safe."

She cast one last glance in the mirror. Snapped a picture with her phone for a keepsake and ran outside.

"You look marvelous!" Miss Louise exclaimed. "If only your boyfriend could see you now!" Ah, if only. "You do have a boyfriend, right?"

"No." She glanced at her profile in the rearview mirror, the Tiffany blue collar framing her face, and wondered who on earth would find her attractive in this dress. Her brown curls began to frizz in the heat.

"Well, that Luke is such a nice young man." Perhaps she thought this because there was a dearth of thirty-something unmarrieds within a fifty-mile radius, but nevertheless, Lily didn't think it was a good idea. "You mean the thought never crossed your mind?"

"We barely get along at times. And besides, we have nothing in common."

Sure, he was good-looking, but not much of a talker.

"Dear, that's what we call spark! Mister Louise and I tussle all the time."

"Mister Louise?"

"He's always dragging his feet to get here and there. I'm always hurrying him up. That's why we gotta go back and pick him up."

When they returned to her house, Mister Louise waited on the porch with his walker.

"C'mon, Mister. We'll be late." She jumped out of the car to help him push the walker just a millimeter faster than he probably would have without her.

"Lily, this is Mister Louise."

"Hi there," she paused, "Mister Louise." It suddenly occurred to her that perhaps Miss Louise's name wasn't really "Louise."

"Well, now Lily, I've heard a lot about you. Thank you for your effort down here. When is Governor Cady coming down to Georgia?" This was the question everyone asked when they first met her. She pleaded ignorance, which was the truth. The campaign never said when. They just said "at some point." A possible visit by Cady was the giant carrot Denver dangled in front of the entire state to get them to work.

"Oh, they haven't told us yet."

"Well, I just can't wait. Can't wait." His wrinkled face appeared seamless in excitement.

"Me neither," Miss Louise chimed in. "I just never, ever, *ever*, thought in my lifetime I'd witness this." Her voice trailed off. She turned her head quickly to the driver's side window, averting Lily's eyes, and brushed a tear off her cheek. The only other time someone uttered those words to her was when a Partner corrected her typos in a finance agreement she had prepared at the last minute for a client. Her eyes were so blurry she missed the commas between the zeros. She squeezed Miss Louise's arm.

The church parking lot was not unlike their office lot, rough gravel with unmarked spaces. The cars blocked each other, indicating that no one left until everyone left. But as the parishioners exited their cars, Sunday church could have been a movie premiere. The hats alone rivaled any red carpet. The gravel lot was soon spotted with turquoise blue fedoras, scarlet red with flowered gauze, and velvet tiger print. She suddenly felt homely in a simple ruffled skirt. People greeted each other with bear hugs and kisses as they caught up on their past week's endeavors. Miss Louise ushered her to the Pastor who stood in front of the church doors, nearly towering over the doorframe himself. He greeted each attendee with an even bigger hug while inquiring into the latest update on their kids' school or their grandparent's health. The tab on his collar tightened with every squeeze.

"Pastor Williams, this is Lily. She works for the Cady campaign."

He smiled even wider than before and cupped her hands with his large fingers. She regretted not getting her nails done.

"Welcome. Oh, this is wonderful. Please join me." And he moved her beside him. Word spread who Lily was, or more importantly, who she worked for, and a line formed to shake her hand. Those who were already seated inside the church returned outside and stood in line again to shake her hand. It didn't matter that she had only tasted oxtail for the first time on Thursday; she worked for Ramal Cady. She wondered whether to confess she didn't have a direct dial to Cady himself, or even his campaign manager, or the deputy campaign manager, but only a revolving office assistant.

Once inside, the Pastor cleared a seat for her in the front pew, despite her insistence that she sit towards the back. "I want to invite you and Miss Louise to sit next to me at lunch today."

Miss Louise grinned. "Oh, thank you. Yes, she would love to."

After he walked to the pulpit, she squeezed Lily's hand and confessed, "I've never sat next to the Pastor at lunch."

"Really? Who usually does?"

"Leaders or sick children."

"You're definitely a leader, Miss Louise. You helped get the volunteers together, provided a space for us to meet. You've helped the campaign from the first day."

"No dear, you're the community leader," she proclaimed with a grin.

The only community leading she had done before this was directing two tourists to the F train. "Oh, I don't know about that."

"Well, you best get ready for your first community speech, because Pastor Williams is about to introduce you." Pastor Williams nodded to Lily, raised his arm for silence, and made his opening remarks to the congregation.

"But, wait, I can't speak up there. I've never spoken in a church. I don't even go to church. Miss Louise, you have to let him know that—"

"Shhh. He's beginning."

"Folks, before we begin our worship, I want you to welcome a very important guest who is here with us all the way from New York City." A rush of whispers temporarily broke the silence. She really wished he hadn't said that. She hadn't found anyone much impressed by her being from New York. "Miss Lillian DeMarco is here on behalf of Governor Ramal Cady." Now the room broke into a fairly loud murmur, with some sporadic squeals, and soft chants of "Cady, Cady, Cady."

"Miss DeMarco, welcome." He beckoned her to the podium. She searched Miss Louise's face for some guidance, and she responded eagerly with a nod. As she walked towards the center she spotted Luke on the other side of the sanctuary wrestling with wires and tools. She immediately felt juvenile, like she was an 11 year old at her first boy-girl dance. She stood before the microphone and stared into the crowd. They anxiously waited for her to speak, as if she were channeling Ramal Cady, or Jesus, on the cross behind her.

"Hi. My name is Lily." She flustered. Now she was 6. "But you already know that." She paused. The faces grew blank. Get it together. "I want to thank you for having me in this beautiful place." She gazed around at the tiny wooden church, which somehow managed to fit nearly 80 people in its shiny pews. The simple white walls with crown moldings hosted faded paintings depicting church goers meeting in barns and open cotton fields. The simplicity was livened by the sea of brightly colored hats.

"As Pastor Williams explained, I work on Ramal Cady's campaign." The audience stirred and she heard the familiar squeals and shouts. "I'm the Regional Field Director for your area, which means I'm responsible for ensuring that every one of Cady's supporters actually votes. This election won't be easy to win, especially here in Georgia." The audience nodded uniformly in agreement. "But, we can win Georgia with everyone's help. So far, I've been working with a few volunteers. Many of you know Miss Louise, who has been a big asset to our team." She directed everyone's attention to Miss Louise who beamed. Mister Louise hugged her shoulders.

"Unfortunately, this past week Miss Louise and the other volunteers were arrested for trying to register voters." That triggered some serious movement in the audience. One person stood up.

"Do you mean they're trying to stop us from voting again?"

"Oh, I didn't mean to suggest that. No, it's just illegal for us to register voters on private property without getting permission from the owner."

"Yep, they sure are," someone else murmured.

"It's just that the volunteers were a little too excited and began registering on SaveAlot's property without permission," said Lily.

"Good for them," piped a male voice from the back row.

"Let's do it again," shouted the lady with the tiger print hat.

"It's actually not good, because now we have this fine to pay," said Lily.

"They're charging us fines again?!" This time the tiger print rose above the neighboring scarlet red hats.

"No, no. It's because they got arrested," explained Lily.

"You see, this is why I don't vote," said the man from the back row

This clearly wasn't going well. The crowd nodded in agreement.

"It's the only store in town. Where else are we going to get registered?" asked the tiger print lady.

"I work over at the poultry farm and those managers tell us no politics allowed. Can't register there either," said a lady sitting in a middle row. She wasn't wearing any hat.

. Lily bit her lip. She wasn't particularly good at pleading. "This is why I need your help. Ramal Cady needs your help. And, well, I need help in posting their bail, which isn't too much."

"How about a fish fry?" suggested the man from the back row. Others spoke up in agreement.

This wasn't the kind of help she had in mind. "A fish fry could work. We are pressed for time, though," Lily responded.

"Yeah, fish fry. Could raise a couple hundred dollars," said the lady without the hat.

"But more importantly, I need help registering the thousands of voters in this region." The audience grew quiet. The exact opposite reaction she hoped for.

"How much does the job pay?" said the tiger print lady.

Lily stood confused. Her eyes darted to Miss Louise, who then nodded for her to answer.

"I'm sorry if I suggested that this was a paid position. We have opened a field office for people to volunteer from. We need volunteers." The audience stirred even more.

"Volunteer, who's got that kind of time? I've barely got time to get to work, feed the kids, and cook." The tiger print lady sat down.

"Volunteer? I thought campaigns pay people to register voters." The man from the back row stood up.

Lily must have appeared completely defeated because she caught a supportive glimpse from Luke. Miss Louise stood up.

"Listen, now I know times are tough and many of you are working two jobs, you're taking care of your kids and your cousins' kids as well. But do you really want to say that in this historic election where we have the chance to get Ramal Cady elected, you sat out? Do you really want your grandkids to know that on Inauguration Day when this country elects its first black President, the most you did was turn on the TV? Please show up Tuesday at the office to help out. However much time you can give." Miss Louise sat down. Mister Louise squeezed her shoulders again. Enough said.

"Thank you, Miss Louise. I will be here after the service if anyone has any questions." Lily slumped off the stage, feeling worse than when she started. Thank God for Miss Louise. Clearly she hadn't been inspiring. Maybe she expected too much. Maybe she just assumed people couldn't wait to be part of the campaign. At least, that's what Wright insisted on the damn conference calls. That there would be droves of volunteers lining up to help. Maybe in Atlanta. Not here in

Ludlow. Maybe she should've warmed up the crowd with "Are you crazy, ready, for Cady?"

As if reading her mind, Miss Louise whispered. "Give it time." This was the more accurate slogan of the campaign.

"How much time? The election is in 5 months." And they were 19,800 registrations short of their goal.

"Have a little faith. They will come." She turned her quiet, confident face back to the pulpit. Pastor Williams returned to the podium and encouraged everyone to volunteer at the Campaign office. Lily flashed a thank you smile and picked up the Bible from the slot in front of her. Maybe a little spiritual inspiration was all she needed.

"Now, let us pick up from last week," Pastor Williams began. "We were speaking of the laws of nature. No person should defy the laws of nature that God intended. When we put forth our own desires before the laws of nature is when we defy God." Another reason to leave further church outreach to Miss Louise.

***

Luke was awake reading a magazine by the porch light when she got home later that night. She hadn't seen him inside the house in a few days. On the night after their jail visit, when she had suggested a late-night snack and beer, he said goodnight in the driveway and retired to his garage apartment.

"Beer?" he asked.

She nodded. He grabbed a frosty bottle from the cooler beside him and flipped the top open. The sky was a dusky blue, and the steam from the afternoon rainfall allowed the smell of fresh cut grass to linger late into the evening. The only sounds for miles were of crickets chirping and kids wrapping up their soccer games. She had grown comfortable with the quiet by now and no longer needed the aid of her sleep machine. She leaned back into the cushioned wicker chair, propped her legs on the cooler, and wondered if it was safe to sleep outside.

She noticed Luke absorbed in his magazine, *Architect's Monthly*.

"Are you an architect?" She had never actually met a real architect before. Only seen them in the movies as the quintessential lead in every romantic comedy.

"I was," he replied. He put down his magazine and propped his legs on the other side of the same cooler. "I'm one of the 40% of the unemployed ones." And this is probably why she had never met an architect in person.

"So now you fix things."

"Yeah. Fix, landscape, construct."

He tossed the magazine aside and reached for another beer.

"I decided to leave Chicago after Dad died. Help my mom. Take a break from the business." His blonde hair glinted in the dusk light. His white t-shirt glowed, outlining the muscles of his chest and masking the grass stains. She suddenly felt mousey. At least she had changed out of her poufy dress and into a t-shirt and blue jeans.

"I've never been," she offered.

"I thought a New Yorker had been pretty much everywhere."

"Except Chicago. And Georgia."

"Yes, except Georgia." He flashed her a smile. He didn't smile often, but when he did, his whole body lifted, as if the gravitational force left him alone for a split moment. He noticed her empty beer and handed her another one. She needed to sip this one.

"Paul, my brother, lives in Houston with his wife and kids. So it made sense for me to come back. Since I don't have either." His eyes lingered a little longer on her and then darted away. They both stared out at the neatly trimmed and landscaped yard before them. Two kids furiously pedaled their bicycles down the street to make it home before dark. If her father died, she would probably move into the basement permanently with her mom.

"It's interesting. Elizabeth just doesn't seem like the helpless type," she remarked. "Are you escaping the mob?" she added jokingly.

He looked at her with shock, like she had just uncovered a secret he struggled to keep to himself. He turned back towards the yard. He wasn't going to answer that question.

She changed the conversation. "I was surprised to see you at church."

"I do some occasional work there. Trying to upgrade their technology and internet."

"I wasn't sure they even had a phone line."

"I'm still working on it. The Pastor's never used email, so it's slow going." She noticed his tool belt resting against the door, the leather worn down so the wrench tipped out of its pocket. She'd never dated a guy who could fix things. Only those who called upon others or just let things remain broken.

"How did the rest of the service go?"

"Well, other than the bout of homophobia, OK. The choir was simply glorious. I'm not religious, but I could listen to a gospel choir any day. They should charge tickets."

"Yeah. I'm a fan of Mahalia Jackson myself. Still have an old record, I think. And a record player buried somewhere in a box. Come over and check it out, when you get a break from the campaign."

"I'd like that."

They resumed listening to the soft street noise. Remaining silent with other guys had always unnerved her. It took a trip to Ludlow, Georgia to make her realize how restorative it could feel.

"I'll admit. I was a little surprised people weren't more willing to volunteer."

"I'm not." The air grew sticky, as the summer breeze settled. He had turned away from her and peered out into the yard. She stared at the outline of his profile — a muscular jaw line, though his teeth were clenched.

"Why?"

"They don't really know who you are yet. Some of them probably are suspicious of whether you actually work for Cady."

"Well, I've got the official badge." She pulled out her paycheck stub. He playfully grabbed it out of her hand.

"Big money," he jibed as he scanned the check.

"Now you know why there is no money for expenses. There's barely any for me." She hoped his attitude toward the campaign would lighten. He gave her a look of disbelief. "So, I'm official." She continued. "Why is everyone here so suspicious? Waiters, gas station attendants, church goers."

"Trust in small towns takes time."

"I just hope it's not too much time."

"That's my point. They know you're here for one purpose, to solicit their help so you win. Help Cady win. Then on November 3rd you'll be gone. And they'll never hear from you again. It's perfectly normal for them to ask if this is some sort of temp job." He squeezed the beer bottle more tightly.

"They don't know that," she defended herself. Then she wondered if that's how he felt. Maybe that's why he was reluctant to open up. He assumed she was leaving. "You don't know that."

"Know what?"

"Know that I'll leave." It was his turn to be surprised.

"Really? You're going to leave New York for good, and move right here to Ludlow where you can get your groceries and your guns at one place?" His lips tightened, and the shape of the lantern reflected in his steel blue eyes.

"Well, no ... but ... I don't know what I'm going to do. I do have this apartment in Manhattan, but ..."

"And?" He leaned forward. His blonde hair fell into his eyes, which he quickly swept back. His t-shirt was damp with sweat. It was past 10 p.m. and the humidity was still stifling.

"I just don't know." She paused. His face awaited a definitive answer. He leaned in closer and she met his lips. She gripped his shoulders and slipped her tongue inside his mouth. He was still for a moment, and she instantly regretted her advance. Then he relented and embraced her willingly, and for a moment she felt certain about her desire, her being at the exact place where she needed to be. For a moment, any doubt about her life subsided.

"What are we doing?" He jumped back and stood up. His eyes darted away from her. "What am I doing?" he muttered and went inside. The screen door slammed shut behind him. She listened to him rummage through the refrigerator and heard the crack of another bottle top open. Rather than return to the porch, he exited through garage door, and returned to his apartment. She saw the light flicker on through the window. Their night was over. She reached into the cooler beside her. Empty. She would apologize first thing tomorrow. He was right. She didn't know what she was doing. And that included him. She grabbed two beers out of the refrigerator and brought them into the bedroom. She finished one and then began to laugh at herself. She'd never made the first move on anyone before. Never. Not even in 4th grade when little girls passed love notes to confused little boys. Being here in Ludlow, away from anyone or anything familiar, all bets were off. Who knew what she would do next?

CHAPTER 11

She woke up the next morning to the pain of her forehead pounding her eyes. She had once chided Gabe for not breaking up immediately with a guy who he discovered drank beer in bed, and now she realized she had been too judgmental. Flanked by two empty bottles and her phone, she opened her eyes long enough to lay the lavender pillow, courtesy of Gabe's care package, over her face and sink further under the covers. Cady would have to forge ahead without her today. She drifted off for a few moments only to be awakened by Gabe's call.

"Got your drunk text."

"I texted you last night?"

"You kissed him!"

"Yes, but it's so awkward. His mother lives down the hall. And he's above the garage. This is weird."

"Awesome."

"What should I do?

"Go right now to his room and kiss him again."

"Gabe, I'm serious."

"OK. Do absolutely nothing. Don't you have an election to win?"

"Yes, and volunteers to extract from jail. I've got to go."

She crawled out of bed, got dressed, and searched for Luke. He had already left for the day. An apology would have to wait.

At the Ludlow jail, she explained to the group that help was on the way. Although a fish fry was in the works, the Pastor had promised to introduce her to their local state Representative who could surely be able to help.

"It's not Robert Winslow, is it?" asked Miss Louise, who had obligingly returned to jail after church in spite of Lily's suggestion that she return home.

"So you know him," said Lily. Miss Louise groaned in response.

"Who is Winslow?" Denise asked.

"Tell him we said thanks," added Ken. Sarah nodded in agreement. "We haven't missed a home game in 12 years and we really need to be out by Saturday." Their Football t-shirts remained clean and unmarred by jail, as if they were used to wearing their shirts every day.

"I don't know Lily. I might wait for the fish fry." Elizabeth suggested.

"We don't have time to wait. He's going to write one big check for all of you. It's much easier this way. Fish fries take time." She had never been to one, but the last she heard, the church group was still brainstorming dates via telephone. She continued her plea. "I've got a big volunteer meeting tomorrow, and I need as many people there as I can get. I'm behind in my goals."

"Lily, it's never as easy at is looks." Elizabeth proclaimed.

She was confident though. "You will all be out by dinnertime." Their faces expressed disappointment to have their jail time adventure come to an end so soon. "The fun will continue out of jail. We have an election to win!" She left to meet their savior.

"I don't think it's a good idea," advised Ford. She had called Ford to update him on the volunteer situation. He still insisted that she find new ones. "We're trying to distance ourselves from the local politicians. Most of them are not helpful. A hindrance really."

If only she could trade places with him just once. She wanted to call the shots from Atlanta and let him bargain for the fine.

"I don't understand. Our volunteers got arrested while trying to help the Campaign. The Campaign won't bail them out, but you won't let another politician bail them out."

"There is no specific rule about this. Just remember, we are not here to help local politicians. We are here to win Georgia for Cady."

"Right. We just want their help."

"Lily, if I need to remind you again …"

"No, you don't. Any update on an AC unit? I've got one fan which barely cools the air to 80. And, how about another order of paper and supplies?"

"I'm working on it." The same answer as the last time she asked. When she had asked Rachel, she suggested a community building exercise of constructing an AC from scratch. "I've got a few reams of paper and pens for you. Will give it to Sam and Parker to take back out there." She rarely saw those two out in Ludlow, since they never moved out here.

She drove along Highway 16 until she reached the turnoff at Jemmy's Joint. At least she would have her key people out of jail shortly. The Representative's office doubled as a real estate office in a largely empty, but newly constructed outdoor esplanade lined with magnolia trees. It was almost noon, and her car was the only one parked in the lot. Not a customer in sight at the sub sandwich shop next door.

"May I help you?" the receptionist asked as she entered the real estate office. She waved an old plastic fan to keep cool.

"I'm here to see Robert Winslow." Lily explained. "I'm Lily DeMarco."

"You mean Representative Winslow?" she corrected.

"Yes."

"Do you have an appointment?"

"No." She double checked to make sure no one else was in the room. "Pastor Williams suggested I come by."

The receptionist dialed the internal intercom, though his door was wide open.

"Yes, Miss Jenkins, please send Miss Day-Marco in," he said into the phone, though she could see him from the doorway.

"You may go in." She finally had permission. She walked into a splendor of office décor: a plush print rug with two leather visitor arm chairs, a polished desk which looked heavier than her car, and a matching cabinet with glass doors displaying framed pictures of Robert Winslow and other politicians. The air was also at least 10 degrees cooler inside the office than in the reception area. She empathized with Miss Jenkins.

"Hello, Miss Day-Marco," Robert said as he took her hand. "Please sit down." Still holding her hand, he led her to the chair. She sunk into it, realizing her old law office never had such accommodations.

"It's actually DuhMarco. No emphasis on the De."

He stared at her for a moment. "Would you like something to drink? Coca-Cola?"

"I'm fine. Thanks." He buzzed the intercom. "Miss Jenkins. Please bring in one Coca-Cola." She could hear the quick open and shut of what could only be a dorm-sized mini-fridge. Miss Jenkins came in, poured the soda can into a glass and placed glass and can side by side on his desk.

He took a sip of Coke as it if it were Scotch. "How are you enjoying yourself here in Ludlow?"

"It's been good. Definitely a change from New York, but the people have been very nice and we're working pretty hard. We're going to win. Georgia is the new Ohio!" She had her campaign speach almost pitch perfect.

"Good to hear." He nodded. "Good to hear." He then reclined back and propped his feet on the desk. "So what can I do for Governor Cady?"

"Oh. Well, I'm actually here about the volunteers. They were arrested for trying to register voters outside of SaveAlot. And, I need to get them out." He looked completely shocked.

"I know. It's crazy that they would be arrested, but SaveAlot is private property and Pastor Williams suggested—"

"You're asking me for bail money?" He interrupted.

Now she was surprised. She thought he knew. He broke into laughter, the kind that ran a full octave from high to low, and then with an abrupt stop pulled his feet off the desk and leaned in to her.

"Now, Miss DeMarco. Let's get to the important details. When will you have some of that Cady money for us?" She was confused.

"I'm sorry. What do you mean?"

"Cady campaign money. For us down here in Georgia." He sounded as if she should know, but she didn't.

"I still don't know what you're talking about. There isn't any money." She barely had money for ink. He squinted suspiciously at her.

"There's plenty of money, Miss DeMarco. It just ain't here."

"I'm here." He slid back into his chair. He surveyed her closely, pausing at the Cady t-shirt and jeans she wore.

"You know my daughter, Susan, her dream is to go to Julliard one day."

"Uh … That's a fine school."

"And she needs these piano lessons. Mighty pricey. And times are tough. Not a lot of real estate sales down here."

She began to fidget in the chair. A nervous habit she picked up working at the firm when Mr. Davies asked for her to take on just one more deal on top of the 18 she already had. She never could say no.

He looked away casually at the door and then back at her. "How about personal? Do you have any personal money?" He said it without flinching. "It would be a loan of course."

She met his eyes and slowly shook her head no.

"I came here to ask you for help. Some of your constituents are in jail for registering more voters in your district. Voters who if they vote, will vote for Cady as well as you." He first looked surprised at her defiance and then his face softened.

She tried to control her anger. She had come to him for help, and now he was asking money from her. What kind of representative was this, and who exactly did he represent? She recalled from her intern days with Weissman, when constituents had called the office, they either tried to help them or told them who else to call for help. She looked around the office. Winslow didn't have any interns. He didn't have anyone but Mrs. Jenkins.

"Miss DeMarco, please don't misunderstand me. In every major election, candidates provide us local folks with money to ensure people have the opportunity to vote. It's the way things work." He leaned back in the arm chair, proud to have explained the world to her.

"Mr. Winslow." She didn't think he deserved the Representative title. "I'm the person who is paid on behalf of Cady's campaign to organize this region so that every one of his supporters votes." She looked at him squarely. "And, frankly, I'm not paid all that much."

"I knew there was something different about him. He don't like to play by the rules." Winslow sighed and emptied the can of Coca-Cola into the glass. "How do you expect to do this?"

"Mostly through a volunteer effort. We have a campaign office where volunteers can make phone calls. We will canvass on the weekends." This time he laughed even harder than before.

"Volunteer? You're not from here. And by here, I mean Georgia. You're not from Atlanta are you? I know you're not from Georgia."

"No." She confessed.

"For the last 30 years, it's always been done the way I explained. Doesn't matter who was running. Black or white. Republican or Democrat. I love all y'all idealistic Northerners who come to the South to try and change things. It's cute." She really didn't like him. "Is there anything else you wanted to talk about?"

"No. Thanks for your time." She abruptly got up and walked out of the office. She breezed past Miss Jenkins who cheerfully exclaimed, "Come back and see us soon."

Elizabeth was right. And as much as she hated to admit, so was Ford. Ashamed to go back to the jail empty handed, she procrastinated at Latte Da for an hour trying to plot her next steps. She had the savings to bail them out, even though it was against Elizabeth's principles. She wouldn't tell them who paid for it, just "a generous local supporter." Not Ludlow local. A generous supporter in Atlanta. She would just have to make this work. They still had 19,765 registrations to go.

She marched over to the deputy's desk and pulled out her checkbook.

"This is confidential, right?" she asked. "No one needs to know who paid."

"We just keep it for our internal records." She spotted the handwritten ledger on the desk. "But, ma'am, it's not necessary." He pushed the check away.

"What do you mean?"

"They were released about five minutes ago. Just dealing with paperwork."

"Huh?"

"Representative Winslow took care of it."

"Huh?"

"He took care of it."

"Well, give him back his money. We don't want it. I'll pay for it." She insisted. She did not want any of his help. Ever.

"Just hold on there, ma'am. Hold on to that money. He didn't pay anything."

"Well, what happened?"

"He called the Sheriff, the sheriff called me and told me to let them go. That's all I know." Or that's all he was willing to say. She wanted to pry further, but the group came out from the back and greeted her with warm hugs.

"Need to call my son and tell him my bail has been posted," Ken boasted.

James urged the deputy to take a mug shot of him as a souvenir. Denise was relieved to see all the contents of her Chanel bag were exactly how she left them.

Elizabeth took her aside. "So what did you have to do to get us out?"

"Actually nothing. I guess Mr. Winslow pulled some strings." Elizabeth gave her a quizzical look. "I really don't know what happened. When I left his office, I didn't think he was going to help us. By the time I got back, you guys were out." She spared her the details.

"Well, it's good to get back on track."

Yes it was, she thought. They had a big volunteer event tomorrow and as usual she was nervous that no one would show. The campaign lived and died on whether people showed up. Ford would want exact numbers of volunteers, registrations, and confirmed sign-ups for the next event. What if no one other than her normal crew came? They would never have enough manpower to meet their goals.

"Come on, dear," Elizabeth embraced her shoulders. Lily welcomed the hug and avoided telling her that Lily had overstepped her hospitality by taking advantage of her drunken son.

CHAPTER 12

After an early dinner with Elizabeth, Lily set off to meet with the so-called Ryan Democrats at their local county meeting. Ford had insisted she make one step toward her persuasion goal, convincing a certain percentage of them to vote for Cady. So far, not a single one of them had attended her volunteer meetings, made a phone call, or knocked on a door.

She arrived 15 minutes late. The back room of the Golden Corral smelled of canned ham and candied peaches. A short man with a protruding belly dressed in blue jeans, collared shirt with bowtie, and cowboy boots, stood before the group and announced the agenda for the evening. Lily was next after the vote on the fall picnic location. There were two choices: the park at Springdale Elementary or the park behind SaveAlot. The SaveAlot park won by a margin of 2 votes.

At the break, the man walked over to her. "Hello, Miss DeMarco. Tasso Day."

He shook her hand firmly.

"Mr. Day. Nice to meet you. I'm glad to be here. The campaign definitely wants to include all Democrats here in this region. We could certainly use your help."

"Yes. I'm sure. We've been busy running the business of the local party here. I know there are some members who have some questions for you."

"I'm happy to answer them."

"Great. Well let's get started. Fellows. Oh, and ladies." He smiled. "I didn't mean to leave you darlings out. Well now, Miss Lily DeMarco is here to speak with us. She's from the Cady campaign."

Lily walked to the center of the room. She was growing more comfortable being in the center of the room, so long as she didn't have to speak or answer any questions. She scanned the room, the men leaned forward so they could hear better, and the ladies picked their peaches with their forks. No one seemed crazy, ready for Cady.

"Hello. I first want to let you know that we have a campaign office just a few miles from here, and I'd love it if you could all attend our volunteer meeting tomorrow."

The room remained silent. She could hear the forks scrape the plates.

"Miss, are you able to answer some questions for us on behalf of Cady?" asked a man dressed strikingly similarly to Tasso, but of slender build.

"Sure."

"Well, I'm worried about my guns."

"What about them?"

"I hear Cady wants to take them away."

"I don't think he's even thinking about your guns."

"But I read—"

"Don't have any more to say. Next question." She poured a glass of iced tea.

"Miss?" Another similarly dressed man, but without a bowtie, raised his hand. She indicated for him to ask his question. He paused, retreated back into his chair, and glanced quickly at his wife sitting next to him. She nodded in encouragment.

"Miss, people are saying he's not really Christian. He follows some ancient Indian ritual of smoking leaves every morning."

Lily coughed up her sweet tea. "What? Where did you hear that?"

His wife came to his defense. "We have reason to believe he's not Christian. Apparently he comes from an Indian tribe."

"Yeah, I hear that if he's President, he's going to take away my land and give it back to the Indians. Something called Imminent Domain."

"Eminent Domain," Lily corrected.

"So you are aware of this plan?"

"No. Yes. No — I'm aware of a legal process called Eminent Domain. But there is no such plan to take away your land."

"What will he do with Imminent Domain then?"

"He's not going to use *Em-i-nent* Domain. The courts do that. I think we are veering off track."

"Do you think his religious background is off base?"

"No. But I can assure you Ramal Cady is a Christian."

"I heard from my sister whose friend works for Eaves that his grandfather was one of those original Indians. They have proof."

"I'm not really sure what to say to that, except these questions are a little ridiculous." She knew coming here was a bad idea. She'd rather just try and win without these people.

"Are you saying we're ridiculous?"

"No, not you but some of these questions—"

"We are all Christians here."

She wanted to throw the pitcher of sweet tea across the room.

"Does it really matter? Tell me, does it really matter if he's Christian, Muslim, Jewish, or whatever that Native American religion you think he belongs to, when a textile mill just closed down the street and left 800 of you unemployed? Does it matter to you that gas prices are $4.20 a gallon and you have no other option but to fill your tanks? Cady doesn't care about your guns. Ask yourselves if you are asking the right questions for you."

The room immediately fell silent. After a minute, people collected their belongings and bid farewell to each other. Tasso Day quickly thanked her for coming and she just as quickly left the building.

"You said what?" Ford screeched on the phone. "Ramal Cady is Christian. Go back in there and assure them of that."

"I did tell them that."

"You also said it didn't matter what religion he was. It absolutely does matter, Lily. What is wrong with you?"

"Ford, they were ridicuolus. I mean Imminent Domian. Returning the lands to the Native Americans. C'mon!"

"I don't care what they ask. You never ever suggest that their questions are stupid. You also never say religion doesn't matter. EVER. Do you understand that? Please tell me you do. Otherwise, I may have to recommend you for something else."

"I understand."

CHAPTER 13

Sam and Parker arrived early to help prepare the office. Sam scrubbed the bathrooms, Parker cleared the recent dead roaches, and Lily re-patched the broken window with fresh duct tape. They worked efficiently for three hours, passing the single bottle of cleaner with the precision of professional basketball players. Each one covered his or her section of the room, priming it for the largest volunteer event so far. They had made nearly 300 calls the night before from the VAN, urging people who lived within a twenty-five mile radius to attend. Some grumbled at the cost of such a trip, as gas had now risen to $4.50 a gallon, but they had assured the potential volunteers that their quarter tank would be worth it. Lily needed more volunteers than her usual six to show up. If they didn't, then it would be game over by July. She shined the beak of the bald eagle lamp her mother had sent, quietly pledging her patriotism.

"Do you want to have a quick meeting to review our goals, before everyone gets here?" Lily asked.

"Sure." They replied in unison. Sam made coffee and Parker unearthed a bag of gourmet popcorn made with real cheese from her backpack. Lily salivated.

"Where did you get that?" At Gabe's urging she had searched the corner gas station, discount general store, the supermarket and even SaveAlot for gourmet popcorn, lemon-lime seltzer, and organic fruit and nut bars to no avail. Cheetos, Snickers, and the occasional late night drive to Chick N' Bik had become her go-to stress snack, a practice which Gabe had threatened to stop by coming down to Georgia himself. His vegan care package sat unopened beneath her desk.

"Atlanta!" Parker gushed. She would find the time to drive into the city. A month ago Atlanta seemed like New York's step-cousin, and now it was the seat of the Roman Empire. Sam gave Parker another adoring look. Lily's mind trailed off to her kiss with Luke. They still hadn't spoken about it. They hadn't even seen each other. She was gone before he awoke for work and in bed by the time he came home.

"Let's hope the 30 volunteers show today. That's how many we confirmed last night, right?" she asked.

"Yup," replied Parker.

"If they each register 10 voters in 2 hours then we will have 300 registrations." Sam added.

"I agree. Let's give them 10 as a goal. That's hard around here, since they'll have to go door to door. Of course 300 doesn't get us too close to 10,000," she lamented. "But baby steps are good. We want them to come back."

"10 registrations per volunteer is too low," Ford commented on their conference call before the event. "Southwest Georgia's goal is 40 per volunteer. Yours should be the same."

Lily was annoyed. "Southwest Georgia has an office that holds a hundred people, twenty phone lines, and an air conditioner." Both Sam and Parker stared at her quizzically wondering how she knew this. "Rachel," mouthed Lily.

"How?" Parker whispered.

Lily muted Ford. "Rich local donor who financed it directly himself."

"We are not going to win at that low goal," Ford insisted.

Lily unmuted. "I'll try and push a higher goal."

107

"We can't." Sam explained after she hung up with Ford. "We don't want to scare them off."

"Good luck with that," said Parker and reapplied her lipstick.

She wanted them to return week after week to volunteer, but she had to push them harder. A lot of time was spent hovering over the snack table of donuts and chips. She needed to get them out the door as quickly as possible, even if it meant dangling the chocolate frosted ones from across the street.

The three of them waited anxiously as the clock struck 2 p.m. Elizabeth and Miss Louise arrived promptly and gave reassuring glances that today's event would bring in more volunteers. And they were right. Nearly forty people showed up to the meeting. Some came from the church, prompting Miss Louise to shoot Lily an "I told you so," which Lily proudly received. James recruited his fellow band members of *Reign Dominion*. Kent and Sarah coaxed members of their bridge club to join by doubling their bids for the next round. Even Denise unearthed two former Republicans from her gated country club community. "We rummaged the local thrift shop for the right clothes," she explained their attire of polyester button downs and tight jeans.

Then, without much coaxing from Lily, the staffers sat with their new recruits and brainstormed about ways to increase their registration efforts. Soon each volunteer teamed up with a partner, and they took their snacks on the go. Her team of six had multiplied into an enthusiastic volunteer battalion, and she watched them proudly as they left the office ready to fan out across the town. She was waving goodbye to the last car in the parking lot, when Luke's truck pulled up beside it. His ordinarily stained white t-shirt was clean and crisp and his hair boasted a neater trim. She hadn't seen him since she kissed him.

"I'm here to fix the bathroom lights," he explained. Elizabeth must've grown tired of using the flashlight.

"Thanks." He walked into the office and she followed behind. He nodded to Sam who was tallying the voter contact counts on the canvass and call data sheets.

"Finally!" Parker squealed at the sight of Luke. Lily would wait for the right moment to say something. Maybe after he fixed the lights. Or maybe over a beer later that night. No, that's how she got here in the first place. Coffee would be better.

"Here's the utility box," she said to Luke. Sooner was always better than later, right? She felt the vibrations of the phone in her pocket. She sent it to voice mail. While later there would be more privacy, it was better just to say it now to avoid any further awkwardness. Her phone vibrated again. Voice mail. She glanced back at the main room. Parker had the keenest ears. She would wait. The phone rang one more time, and this time she just turned it off.

"Oh, Lily. About the other night." He turned to face her.

"Yes," she unexpectantly whispered.

"Well, we had a couple of drinks."

"Yes, too many. I woke up with a headache and couldn't get out of bed, and then with Ford calling—"

"OK, so it was no big deal, right?"

"Lily," Parker called out. "Ford's on the phone for you."

"Guess you need to take that?" said Luke.

"Yeah. I do." He flipped the utility box open and began to play with the switches. She lingered as he continued to flip the switches on and off. It *was* no big deal, right?

"Found it." He said with triumph. "Easier to fix than the roaches."

"What a relief."

"Lily, Ford needs that update on numbers right away."

***

The volunteers returned even more fueled with excitement than when they left. Lily listened attentively as some proudly boasted of the neighborhoods they canvassed without trepidation. Others described with the relish of a cooking show judge the oxtail and collard greens they sampled for the first time at the local soul food restaurant while registering diners. Even visits to the barber shops and beauty parlors, local hardware and package stores, pawn shops and the Dollar General, yielded their own mini-adventures and more registrations than ever before.

"People were so thrilled to see us!" enthused one volunteer. "They saw us with our candidate stickers and registered." Another nodded in agreement.

"Yeah. Some of them had no idea Cady had a local office. They signed up to volunteer next time." James and his friends returned from a high school football practice, where they registered players and their parents. Elizabeth's trip to the local Boys and Girls club yielded similar results.

A lady dressed in a pink sundress and peep toe heels pulled Lily aside during the celebration. Her grey hair was cut short and covered by a wide rimmed hat.

"I saw you speak yesterday."

"At the county party meeting?"

The lady nodded. Lily lowered her eyes.

"I'm really sorry for how I spoke to you guys."

The lady's eyes narrowed. "You definitely didn't care for us, that was apparent." Lily looked away. "But, you did make some sense. And today, I walked through one of those housing complexes owned by the government. What do you call them?"

"Section 8. But they're not really owned by the government. They use vouchers and are regulated—"

"Yes, well ..." the lady nervously scanned the room and then broke into a smile. "I registered 23 people. I couldn't believe it. And let me tell you." She scanned the room again. She leaned into Lily and whispered. "The people I met behaved more princely than some of the people I've known my entire life." She squeezed Lily's arm.

"Thank you," said Lily. "Thank you for surprising me."

The lady rejoined the celebration at the snack table. Lily watched as everyone exchanged stories of the new people they met, brainstormed of new places and those to which they would return, and reveled in their accomplishment of 809 registrations. They celebrated with more Cheetos, Snickers, and Cokes. It didn't matter that forty people squeezed into the shack made it feel like 120 degrees.

"I just want to say how excited we are tonight," she announced, standing on a chair in front of the room. She acknowledged Sam and Parker who looked equally excited. For the first time since she arrived she sensed victory in Georgia. "This is a tough region and what you guys did today surpassed our expectations," she continued. "It's been —"

She was interrupted by the screech of aluminum scraping against linoleum. Representative Winslow appeared at the back of the crowd and sidled to the center of the room. Chairs parted to create an aisle, allowing him to shake hands and pass out his real estate business card. He then stopped at the front, with his back toward Lily, and turned to face the audience like the keynote speaker.

"Miss DeMarco, thank you for all you are doing here in Ludlow," he announced aloud and turned to Sam and Parker. "Are you two working with Miss DeMarco as well?" They nodded and he cupped their hands like a parent acknowledging a child's effort. "Well, thank y'all for the hard work y'all are doing on the campaign down here."

"Mr. Winslow," Lily whispered. "We're wrapping up for the evening. I'm happy to chat with you afterward."

"Miss DeMarco, I'm simply here to say a few words to the people of my district." He grinned. "That's alright with you, I reckon."

She glanced at Sam for an answer and he shrugged. "Sure. Of course. That's fine." She sat down.

"Ladies and Gentlemen, thank you for being here today. We appreciate all y'all's hard work volunteering for Governor Cady."

Parker sighed loudly. Lily shot her an equally annoyed glance and searched for a way to politely interrupt.

"The election here in Georgia will be tough, but it is winnable. With all of your hard work and the community coming together, we can win. Now let's all join hands and pray. Pray for victory."

James nudged one his high school buddies to leave the room, but he was too far from the door. Sam whispered to Lily, "I'm Jewish."

"I know and I'm not religious. Can we just call this a moment of silence?" She asked Sam.

"That's when someone dies," retorted Parker. But she relented, and to Lily's relief, joined hands with Sam and the larger circle.

She cast an empathetic glance to James and his friends, and hoped for no homophobic references. Once this was over she would inform the volunteers of their percent-to-goal, how many more shifts they needed to fill, and the expanded hours the office would be open from then until Election Day. She had a captive audience of 40 volunteers. She couldn't let this moment slip to inform them of the work that lay ahead.

Winslow continued. "Now, I'd like to introduce y'all to someone. He's been working relentlessly to help our candidate. Please welcome Tasso Day, your local County Democratic Chairman." This couldn't get any worse. Tasso sauntered to the front and stood beside Winslow. Tasso, a white man, with straight blonde hair, wearing a button-down, jeans, and cowboy boots, looked the exact opposite of Winslow, a black man wearing a custom fitted suit with cuff links, yet they gestured the exact same way, raising the left hand to quiet the room while using the right to shake people's hands. They both stood erect with their arms by their side after everyone was quiet.

"Thank y'all for letting me speak here tonight." Tasso began. "And thank you, Lily, and others for all the hard work you're doing. I want to tell you the story of an election not too long ago, when Georgia went for a Democratic President." Uh oh. "I met Roy Stafford in 1991 and offered to help him on his campaign here in Georgia." Lily hoped no one could hear Parker groan. "We spent a day preparing my boat, stocking it with beer and other provisions. And from the Augusta Riverwalk, we set sail down the mighty Savannah River to thousands of people cheering us on. We encountered torrential downpour and rough waves, but that didn't stop us. No. Didn't stop us one bit. We anchored at every small town along the river. And at every port, hundreds, and sometimes thousands of people, awaited our arrival. They came from as far away as Tennessee, South Carolina, and Florida. We sailed to the port in Savannah and guess what?" He eyed the crowd who, surprisingly, seemed captivated. "Yep, you guessed it. Thousands of people cheered our arrival."

Thousands of people? She started to fidget. Sam buried his head in his hands. Parker rolled her eyes. The small towns across Georgia cheering the Democratic nominee? Thousands of people just didn't move that fast here.

"That's a very special boat we sailed on. Through tough waters and the occasional protestors, but because of that boat trip and Stafford visiting all those thousands of people, we won Georgia."

And it had nothing to with a third-party candidate siphoning off nearly 20% of the votes. As Day compared himself to Washington crossing the Delaware, Lily forced herself to remain quiet. It would be over soon.

"Afterward, I donated the boat to the Augusta museum, but those artsy people just ain't that smart and refused to take it. I do keep it in my back shed if anyone would like to take a picture with it."

At this point Representative Winslow cleared his throat as a signal to move on. For once, she and Winslow were on the same page. "In summation, the point I was trying to make was that the boat trip was a BIG idea. Campaigns are about Big Ideas. Try and imagine something as big of an idea as that boat trip and I guarantee you," he paused for dramatic effect, "we will win." And with that he began his journey to the back of the room, shaking hands and passing out his business card. Tasso Day: Lawyer, real estate agent, political consultant.

CHAPTER 14

Sam tried to reassure Lily. "Who knows, maybe people were inspired by the story. It's nice to be reminded that we actually once won Georgia." She hoped it was the last she had seen of Winslow and Day, but that was probably wishful thinking. Not that she would ask them for any further help. She just didn't want them getting in her way.

"Yeah, it was all due to a boat ride," retorted Parker.

"We still won." Sam reiterated firmly.

"Barely. By less than 1%, and Stafford still didn't get above 43%. "

"Why can't you just let this go?"

"Because you said we would both return to Boston together and apply to grad school there. Now you tell me you want to travel for the rest of your life?"

"No. Just for a year." He hesitated. "Or two."

Parker slammed the stack of canvass and call data on his desk. "Here. You enter these in."

"Where are you going?"

She turned to Lily. "I need to run an errand. I'll be gone the rest of the afternoon."

Parker marched out the front door. Despite the several hours of work that lay ahead, Sam quietly began entering the data into the computer. This was the first time she'd seen the two of them disagree. They even drove their cars at the same speed.

"I need to go to Atlanta tomorrow. Try and see what I can scrounge up in supplies," Lily said. She refused to ask for any more donations from her volunteers. "Can you hold down the fort?"

Sam nodded, while still focused on the computer screen. She glanced at the screen door. "Alone, if needed?" He nodded again.

. The next day she arrived to a buzzing Atlanta Headquarters, overflowing with campaign paraphernalia. Shipments of yard signs, buttons, bumper stickers, and t-shirts had just arrived. Reams of paper lined the shelves and new computer stations were being installed. To the extent Georgia had anything, it was here in Atlanta. She spotted Tim, in his brightly colored oxford and khakis, shaking hands with members of the mayor's staff and trumpeting his City of Atlanta turf. Angela was tucked away in the corner, steadfastly entering data and double-checking each registration. Tim waved Lily over to his conversation and introduced her to a few of Atlanta's business leaders, union leaders, corporate lawyers, and bankers who had all made their way to the office offering to volunteer or donate. Everyone smiled or laughed, as they rejoiced in the jubilant atmosphere that promised victory. The doubt that Cady could lose hadn't crossed anyone's mind.

"If you ever want to volunteer out in Ludlow, we'd love to have you." She told a man sporting a tailor-made business suit and gold cuffs.

"Ludlow?" He asked. "I'm not even sure I know exactly where that is."

"It's a couple hours outside the city. But if you don't want to come in person, we could definitely use a couple of computers. And the office is so hot. We could use an AC unit." Tim shot her a stern look. She would scramble for whatever she could get. She had no shame in groveling.

"Oh. Well, that's not really Atlanta."

"No, I guess not." She was in the other Georgia where Cady supporters hid in the closet equipped only with a fan. Tim quickly ushered the man to the coffee area. She would have to press Ford. If no one in Atlanta wanted to donate an air conditioner, then someone in Denver would have to.

She weaved past groups of volunteers, bypassing Tim's office along the way. She spotted a younger, thinner, and less clothed version of Denise with a spray cleaner and paper towels. She peeked into Rachel's office, but it was empty. A lit cigarette sat on top of a beer can. She dumped it inside the beer and tossed the can. She found Ford and Gianna in Ford's office huddled around a speakerphone talking to Wright. Ford's shirt was untucked; his bow tie lay on the floor. The newly grown five o'clock shadow showed a speckling of stray gray hairs. Potato chip crumbs were sprinkled around him. He leaned into the speakerphone and raised his voice.

"We have 11 offices with no internet or phone lines. How are we supposed to contact voters when we have nothing to contact them with?"

"Hey man," Wright replied, "We love everything you're doing there in Georgia. Fucking amazing, really. It's just taking some time. You'll get them soon." Wright hung up and Ford threw his phone at the wall. Gianna massaged his neck and shoulders in an effort to soothe him.

"We are getting fucked!" yelled Rachel and stormed out of the room. Lily saw Ford slump his head to the table, with Gianna close behind him. She stood in the doorway, not wanting to interfere. After a minute he looked up.

"Lily, what's up?" His voice was listless. He could barely lift his head. She instantly regretted all those secret ill wishes against him and felt the impulse to help, rather than demand more.

"Well, I came to ask for more supplies. We've barely got anything," she said sheepishly.

"Yeah, I know," Ford admitted. Now she was really worried. This was not his usual response of "make do" or "seek donations." "I really am working on it."

"Yeah, I know." She smiled. He grinned in response. Gianna grimaced.

Rachel returned from the room with the end of one cigarette and ready for another.

"You can't smoke that in here," reminded Gianna.

Rachel flicked the lighter on and off, waving the cigarette through the flame. She smirked at Gianna's horror. The nerve center was falling apart. Lily preferred Ford with his authoritative condescension. The four sat around the table in silence for at least five minutes, listening to the murmur of the crowds in the main room. Every moment was filled with constant emails, phone calls, and people, lots of people. Those she hoped to see again and those she hoped to avoid.

Gianna spoke first. "Guys, we're going to win this. Wright says the supplies will be coming, so they will get here. We just keep doing what we're doing."

Rachel shot her a more dampening glance than the one before. "I don't trust him."

"But we have no choice, right now," Ford responded. "Let's continue to parcel out our supplies and get the rest from local volunteers." Lily nodded in agreement. They didn't have a choice. Either that or pack up and go home. And they couldn't go home. Not right now. "We will just let everyone know that supplies are forthcoming. And Georgia is winnable. The same thing we've been saying all along."

Rachel lit up her cigarette. No one said a word.

"Why so glum?" Tim asked, poking his head through the door.

"They're busy working, unlike some people," Angela retorted. Her voice boomed from behind the pile of campaign t-shirts in her arms.

"Girl, I'm working. I just met with a very important volunteer." He grinned.

"The one from the club last night? Or the night before?" Lily wondered if they should just go ahead and sleep with each other. From the first day at the all-staff meeting, they've been at each other's throats. Perhaps it was the stress of the campaign, or the pent-up sexual frustration of working side by side in Atlanta.

"Going to clubs is part of the job," Tim defended. "There are lots of Cady supporters there. I'm getting everyone's number."

Angela threw the t-shirts in his face. "So is folding these." And she stormed out of the room. The iridescent imprint of Cady's profile fell splat against the linoleum floor, which was specked with cola residue. Tim began to brush them off and fold them for the sales table. They all joined him in the effort, slowly creating neatly stacked rows of t-shirts, organized by size and color, to be displayed on the sales table later.

"Supplies still haven't come for the rest of the state," Ford filled Tim in. "Trying to figure out what to do." He refolded a t-shirt three times until on the fourth try, Gianna waved for him to hand it to her.

"Don't you guys worry," Tim answered. "I'm going to win City of Atlanta for us, and when I do, we will win the state."

Lily glared at Tim. "What makes you think that?"

"Most of the supporters are in Atlanta, and we just need to make sure they vote."

"So am I on some sort of tortured vacation out in Ludlow? If so, I'd rather get burnt on the beach."

"Frankly, I'm not even sure where Ludlow is," said Tim.

Lily wanted to throw the nicely folded t-shirts back in his face. "Clearly. The money is here. The volunteers are here. The staff is here. Then what the hell am I doing out in Ludlow?" This time she surveyed both Tim and Ford for answers. "Do you know what it's like trying to unearth Cady supporters from under one rock at a time? Trying to get them to publicly announce their support? It's like getting wives to talk about the sex they're not having with their husbands."

"We still need to win a certain margin in the rest of the state," Ford explained. "We need Atlanta, surely. But we need a certain percentage in the rest of the state, too."

"You see. You can't win Georgia without Atlanta," Tim reemphasized. Lily hoisted a stack of shirts.

Ford intervened. "Lily, we still need those goals met in the rural areas."

"I want an air-conditioner."

"What?"

"I'm not leaving without one."

Ford studied her face for a minute, as if she had just asked for a diamond engagement ring after only two weeks of courtship. Then he relented.

CHAPTER 15

Her worries subsided as she exited off the interstate and on to the state highway back to Ludlow. Even the sprinkling of fast food chains and pawn shops warmed her heart; for she had an air conditioner. No more cool-downs with wet paper towels and a spray bottle. The rickety fans now had additional support. This was a gift from Ford, and though they weren't supposed to pay for supplies and equipment themselves, she would compromise for an air conditioner. If he would buy it, she would take it. After all, it was now July in Georgia, and the air was thick and damp. A rainstorm had passed through without cooling the atmosphere. She could feel the heat emanating off the blacktop. When she pulled into the gravel lot, Sam and Parker cheered. Miss Louise was particularly impressed by the remote control. They sealed the unit in the window with wooden slats and duct tape, and within an hour the temperature grew conducive to a discussion of their next steps in reaching their goal of 18,175 registrations.

"Our region is vast." Sam pointed to the map. "It spans 16 counties stretching south of the North Carolina border and East to the South Carolina border."

Lily moved the bald eagle lamp out of her sightline. "Yes, I know. So what are you saying?"

"We've only really concentrated our efforts here."

"This is the most populous area," explained Parker.

"Well, we need to get further out. Maybe it's time we split up. Divide and conquer."

"I don't know. It makes me nervous. Ludlow is tough enough, but in those far-reaching rural towns, it's normal to carry guns to schools, churches, and the playground," lamented Parker. Lily wondered whether her concern really stemmed from the fact that Parker and Sam had never worked apart.

The door chimed open. "Are you open?"

"Larry, it's Sunday. The liquor store is closed," Lily replied. He bowed his head and took off his baseball cap.

"Thank you, ma'am."

She examined the map. Sam was right. They would have to scatter across the region and squeeze out every last registration across the little towns, since they couldn't reach the people on their weekend trips to SaveAlot.

Sam embraced Parker's shoulders. "It'll be fine. We just head out during the day. We'll meet back here afterward." She seemed reassured and the two began to divide up the territory.

Lily sorted through the pile of mail. She was surprised that people even knew the office address. Apparently the county paper's news report did get some traction. Ford had congratulated her on the "earned media." Not having to pay for advertising went along the campaign theme of not having to pay for anything. She sorted through the letters and began to open the packages intended personally for Cady, but which would stop right here in Ludlow. She popped in a CD by a local rap artist. "For your consideration to be played at inauguration," read the note.

Turn Georgia Blue,
Turn Georgia Blue,
Turn, Turn, Georgia Blue
Turn Georgia Blue

Simple, but with a catchy beat overlaid by Cady's speech. Not bad, she thought. She slipped the disc into her "Keep" pile.

She popped in another disc
Well there's people and more people
What do they know know know.
Go to work in some high rise
and vacation down at the Gulf of Mexico
John Cougar Mellencamp's Pink Houses covered by a local bluegrass singer and her banjo. Still relevant twenty years later. Keep.

The rest of the mail was handwritten letters.

Dear Candidate, I have fought for three generations for marijuana rights, now more than ever is the time for the rights of marijuana seekers
Toss.

Dear Candidate, Enclosed is $100 from our church as a donation.
Return.

People's Rally, Saturday. Noon. Backstage. Monroe, Georgia.

"Where is Monroe, Georgia?" she asked Sam.

"Just south of here. It's in our region and we need to cover it. Why?"

"Well, I'll take Monroe," she suggested, and handed him the flyer.

"OK. I'm headed due north into the mountains," he announced.

"You can register as you belay."

"I hope my harness doesn't break. Parker is headed to a festival east of here." Parker nodded nervously.

"What kind of festival?"

"It's the Elbert County Festival. Elizabeth heard from her mechanic there was something going on over there," Parker explained.

"It'll be good to get out of our comfort zones," said Lily.

"Coming to Georgia was stretching my comfort zone," Parker sighed. She had a point.

***

Lily set off early on Saturday. She had googled Monroe County, Georgia as her organizing handbook suggested. *Google is a tool to learn about a town and its top highlights. This allows an organizer to learn what the town considers important. And, it is an entry point to mutual understanding.* Her search revealed a list of antebellum homes on the state historical preservation list and that Monroe was home to the largest skydive club in Georgia. If she hit her goal, maybe she would try jumping from a plane. But only if she met the goal. One registration less, she was out. She drove down even smaller roadways than in Ludlow, passing through beautifully preserved small towns populated by pecan trees and plantation houses that Sherman must've refused to burn. Monroe's main street was lined with quaint country stores selling jams and antiques, a large red brick community center where an afternoon show was scheduled, and a small café serving tea and biscuits. Townspeople strolled the streets in their finest suits and bowties, and girls donned frilly frocks. She couldn't find the *Backstage* or any sign of the People's Rally, and flagged down a young man wearing a coat, bowtie, top hat, suspenders, and brandishing a cane. *Be nice,* she reminded herself, *He doesn't need to know that he looks like Charlie Chaplin. You just need directions.*

"Hi there. Do you know where the Backstage is?" The man removed his hat and lowered his eyes. One of his suspenders popped loose and he quickly refastened them.

"Ma'am. Can you please ask that again?"

"Have you heard of the Backstage?"

"We have a *main* stage. It's right there." He pointed. "It's our annual town Antebellum Brunch." Not exactly a civil war reenactment that Gabe warned about, but not that far off base. Clearly not a setting for the People's Rally. The only times she had dressed up for brunch was at a friend's wedding. She much preferred the casual Sunday approach in jeans with pancakes, bacon, and mimosas.

"Let me clarify. I work for Ramal Cady and I am looking for the People's Rally." She showed him the flyer. "It's supposed to be in Monroe."

"Mon-row," he corrected. "Not Munroe."

"Mon-row then," she said.

He suddenly looked directly at her. "It's probably over there somewhere" and pointed to a road that tapered off into dirt. "I'm voting for the other guy." He strolled off twisting his cane in the air. Yes, that she knew. After her meeting with the Ryan Democrats, she knew there was nothing that she could to do to persuade certain people to vote for Cady. Her "to do" list now included finding an alternative to the persuasion phase. Her only idea so far was to plant a news story that Eaves was Mexican.

The dirt road ultimately led to a gravel lot where she noticed a wooden picnic shelter and a line of bleachers in the distance. Her trusty Volvo held up just fine. The music of a Cajun blues band thumped as she walked closer, the smell of hot dogs emanated from the charcoal grill, and she spotted two ladies selling silk-screened homemade Cady t-shirts and posters displaying the requisite portraits of MLK Jr., JFK, and Cady, but this time with Jesus hung from the cross instead of Gandhi. Many others had tokens of Cady paraphernalia on sale, too; hats, socks, belt buckles, homemade soap, and candles with a special Cady musk scent. A whole cottage industry kept the locals afloat. Lily watched the crowd milling around the picnic tables and card tables and salivated. There had to be at least 100 people, some white but mostly black; the most she'd seen anywhere in her region come together in support of Cady.

She approached the t-shirt ladies and offered to buy one. Hot pink with Cady's face outlined in black.

"What's your name?" one of them asked. She displayed two versions of Cady. One with a hand on his chin in deep contemplation; the other with a wide smile. The lady's own smile was just as wide.

"Lily." She pointed to the smiling Cady. "I'll take this one."

"Oh, you're that lady working for Cady!" the other responded. "Hey y'all," she yelled to those seated on the benches. "This is Cady's people. C'mon over." People rushed over to speak with her. They gave her cards and gifts to pass along to Cady himself. An elderly man stumbled over, leaning heavily on his cane.

"Hello, Miss. My name is Eldridge Holley." He delicately clasped the fingers of her hand, turned it over, and placed two registration forms in them. "Please take these forms. We're registering for the first time and didn't want to just put them in the mail."

"Thank you, sir. I'm happy to take them." She liked his formality. He also wore a bowtie and suspenders with his suit, but they fit his bulging belly perfectly.

"We tried to register many years ago, before you were born, but weren't allowed to. Then we just stopped trying. But, we decided to try again."

She wanted to squeeze him in a bear hug. "I'll make sure these get delivered to the right place." He tipped his hat and stumbled back to his seat.

A dashing young teenager eagerly ran up to her with his form in hand. He wore a suit that was about two sizes too big for his skinny build. "I'll be 18 exactly on Nov. 1st. I cannot wait to vote."

"Me, too," she replied. He held a notepad and pen close to him. "What are you working on?"

"My speech. I'm running for Senior Class President." He barely looked old enough to drive.

"I was on Student Council myself at your age."

"Wow. And now you get to work for Cady! My cousin told me it was stupid to run. But I gotta tell him you did it and now look where you are." He darted toward a heavier kid who was dancing in front of the band. She was flattered by her first and only fan.

More people registered to vote, others danced to the music with hot dogs in one hand and beer in the other, and a few others, like her, just absorbed the celebration. As she milled around looking through the wares, her face brushed a noose that hung by a nail from the rafters. It floated above the table; its loop the perfect size for Lily's head. She quickened her step past the table.

"You're that Cady person." An old man lounging low in a folding chair a few feet behind the table forced her to stop.

"Yes." His leathery black skin did not square with being a KKK member.

"The reenactment is July 25th." He pointed from his lounge at the flyers lying on the table. She obliged. The cut was uneven and the handwritten print was difficult to read.

"Reenactment?"

"The unsolved murders, lynchings, of Mr. and Mrs. Larry and Dorothy Randall, and Mr. and Mrs. George and Mable Dixon. Occurred just a mile from here. Over on Moore's Ford Bridge. 1946. No suspects. No investigation." He paused and peered up from underneath the bill of his cap. "Miss Dorothy was pregnant, you know."

"Dorothy? The woman who was …"

"Yes. Her." She didn't know. She didn't even know about the unsolved murders. How come it didn't show up on her Google search? He needed a megaphone. He needed to tell someone important. He needed a 30 minute television ad on Best American Lip Sync. How is it that no one knew? The lettering on the pamphlet came into clearer focus. "Monroe, Georgia; Home of the last known mass lynchings in the United States." She felt his expectations through his piercing gaze.

"Will you come to the reenactment?" he asked.

"Well, it's just that I'm so busy with the campaign. I have to meet these registration goals, and …" Her voice trailed off, even though he didn't interrupt her. She felt silly trying to make excuses.

"I understand. You've got a lot on your plate working for Cady."

She was the closest this man had probably ever come to a Presidential Candidate of the United States and she could offer nothing. She was just a former corporate lawyer who was treading water until a better opportunity presented itself. She couldn't get a second kiss from Luke. She still had to beg her own volunteers for paper. It took her two months to secure an air-conditioner.

She flipped through the handwritten pamphlet.

"Sir?"

"Call me Stan."

"It's nice to meet you, Stan."

"I didn't say that was my name. Just said you could call me Stan."

She hesitated. "OK. Stan? If you'd like, I'd like to type this flyer for you. Make it a little easier to read. Maybe add a couple of photos and print you some copies."

His eyebrows furrowed and he looked away. He pondered the offer silently for a minute, gazing at the revelry over by the band.

"I'd appreciate that." His cracked smile revealed large, tarnished, crooked teeth. "My handwriting is pretty messed up." And then his smile broke into a deep raspy laugh, sounding more like a cough.

She smiled in relief.

"Thank you for working for Cady down here in these parts. I just never thought in my lifetime I'd witness a black man as a real contender. I'm still unsure about all this."

"Yes, I know." She understood why people were circumspect of her effort. She now understood why there were those who didn't believe, or if they did believe, did so cautiously. She had read enough of Lovell's memoir to understand why rural black southerners would be suspect of any political party. The Democratic Party in the south hadn't welcomed blacks for generations. It was fairer to say they had been outright excluded. And even when they tried, in the fateful summer of 1964, to hold their own elections and be seated at the national convention, the national party denied them as well. And the Republicans weren't even around. She had stumbled upon old laws which still remained on the books, unintentionally maybe, and probably not enforced, but county commission seats that required candidates to be property owners. She received reports of people without transport having to travel 12 miles to their polling location, because the one nearby had closed. And some were forced to vote in the churches of preachers who publicly questioned Cady's citizenship. Even now, she wasn't naïve. She knew it would take luck, money, and a black man who people wanted to drink a beer with, or a woman who people wanted to screw, to elect either as President. And someone like Gabe had no chance. It wasn't until now where she was in a battleground state, where history outlived progress, that she realized the unprecedented work it would take to make this a reality.

She eyed the jubilant crowd again as they danced, sang, ate, and extolled Cady with their homemade signs. This must be what Lovell meant when he referred to the "Marrow of a Movement," the most essential part of an endeavor for change, which contains an inexorable force to which people simply surrendered. The young man running for class president, the couple registering to vote for the first time, and the two ladies designing their own version of Cady campaign t-shirts were all swept up in the marrow of change. Just like Lily, they had hitched their wagons to something larger than themselves. Something greater than Monroe and its history, their ordinary lives on the other side of the railroad tracks. There at the crossroads of a dirt path and a gravel lot hidden by fields, she realized that losing simply just wasn't an option. No matter what happened, they had to win. No matter what it took and by any means necessary.

Parker texted from her Elbert festival. *Amzin Met biker gang Lots of voter regs*

#? Lily texted in response.

22

Need 20 more

She checked her Blackberry and emailed Sam with a similar demand.

The music stopped as a man, not much older than 40, walked onto the stage and took the microphone off the stand. He wore a simple collared blue shirt, tan slacks and a corduroy blazer, unaffected by the heat. Lily swatted away the mosquitoes. Thankfully, Gabe's natural care package had also come with Bug Off, which became her new scent for the summer. The gentleman cleared his throat.

"Ladies and gentlemen. My name is Lowell Quarterman." The crowd quieted down.

"I operate the funeral parlor over there on MLK Drive. Many of you know it." There were lots of nods. "Funeral work has been part of my family for years. My grandfather was an embalmer. My father was the funeral director. And I've continued on with their legacy. I thoroughly enjoy my work. And I've always been happy with this work." He paused and the crowd remained attentive.

"But this past year, I was inspired to do something more. Take this work to the next level. Try and serve the greater Monroe area community with my skills. Which is why I've decided to run for Monroe County Coroner." The crowd cheered him on.

"We all," he pointed to himself and the crowd. "We all have had a history of sitting out of public service here in Monroe County. And I understand why. But we can no longer continue to sit out." *No* came from the crowd. "We must get involved." *That's right. Yes, we must.* "Y'all all know people who sit out. Our brothers, sisters, sons, daughters, aunts, uncles, cousins, and our parents." Lily nodded in unison with the crowd. "We can't let them sit out this year." *No we can't.* "We must encourage them. Inspire them. Explain to them why they can no longer sit out. Take them to the polls!" *Yes* shouted the crowd. *Yes, Take them,* Lily mouthed aloud. *Please take them.* "Take them by their hands and take them to vote. For when they vote, we will have a new President and a new County Coroner."

The crowd roared and began to chant. *Take them. Take them. Take them.*

"Now, I'd like to introduce Miss Lillian DeMarco, who is here working on behalf of Governor Ramal Cady. She'd like to say a few words as well."

The chants drifted into silence as the crowd eagerly awaited her speech. Lowell Quarterman had been plenty inspiring and she quickly considered whether there was a way for her to bow out. But Lowell was beckoning her to the stage, and the crowd grew noisy in anticipation. This was the largest crowd she'd spoken to since the church episode, and she hoped her persuasion skills had marginally improved. Lowell handed over the microphone and squeezed her hand in reassurance. She held it close to her mouth and shouted "Hello!" only to hear resounding feedback which caused the crowd to jump back. At least they were alert.

"Hello, everyone. As Mr. Quarterman explained, I work for the Cady Campaign." While she heard the usual applause, it seemed to her that this time the faces anticipated more than typical campaign speak, as if she could reach Cady on speed dial. How could she top Lowell Quarterman? She couldn't. She would finally do it. That annoying warm-up speech.

"Are you crazy?" The crowd looked askance. Some shook their heads no. Maybe it started with ready instead of crazy.

"Are you ready?" This time many nodded and shouted some yeahs. Ok, the crowd seemed to be warming up.

"Are you crazy, ready for Cady?" Some yeahs. Some looked around in alert, waiting for Cady to appear.

"Good job, everyone. I'm really excited to be here. You are all a crucial part of winning here in Georgia. We can really win here. But as Mr. Quarterman emphasized, we need to take everyone to the polls!" The crowd murmured slightly as she repeated Mr. Quarterman's statement. Maybe she needed to emphasize it more. Speak louder.

"I'll be taking people." She paused for effect.

"You'll be taking people." She spoke even louder for effect.

"And together we will take everyone to the polls!" She did garner a few claps and some coughing from the back.

"Well, thank you for having me." And she exited the stage.

"You did fine." Lowell assured. His warm brown eyes exhibited sincerity.

"I was awful, but I survived," she said. "I'll never get used to making speeches. But Mr. Quarterman, you were amazing. Really."

"I really want to win," he said. "I think I could make a damn good coroner."

"I think you would make a damn *great* coroner." She whispered in his ear as she hugged him goodbye.

CHAPTER 16

She arrived at the Atlanta headquarters for the 9:30 a.m. statewide meeting Ford had scheduled on one day's notice. On the conference call the night before, Ford provided the latest update on each region's percent to goal numbers. Everyone was behind. He summoned everyone to Atlanta to reveal an important new statewide strategy. She was ready for a winning formula *and* an increased budget. The room was already filled with organizers from around the state scavenging for pens, staplers, lingering reams of paper, and unclaimed campaign chum. She spotted Sam and Parker cornering two boxes of paper against the backside of a computer desk. Sam carried the boxes out the back door, while Parker served as lookout. Lily nodded in approval.

She surveyed the room, which was now packed tightly with organizers from the bigger cities of Savannah, Augusta, Albany, and Macon, as well as the, outer-lying areas of the affluent 'Burbs of Atlanta and New Bethel in Middle Georgia. No longer did they have the previously donated office space from Talmadge & Adair LLP. The organizers now filled the hallways, desks, back offices, and even stood outdoors with the door propped open. The staff had morphed into the personalities of the turfs in which they lived and worked. Team

Savannah came outfitted in trucker hats, newly grown facial hair, and fresh tattoos, resembling the students at the major art school there. Those from Albany — pronounced Al-Binny — were dressed in overalls and canvas slip-ons, as if they had stepped out of *Huckleberry Finn*, ready to set sail upon a wooden raft down the Flint River. Lily took stock of her own attire, as well as Sam and Parker's. The three of them wore jeans, over-sized t-shirts, and baseball caps.

Tim and his entourage regaled the rest of the organizers with their experience of filming a rap video on behalf of Cady with Young Queasy and D.Y. Angela still served as his conscience; piping in to remind him of all the time he didn't spend reaching out to voters. The 'Burbs discussed the benefits of shrimp over smoked salmon at their catered phone banks and debated the verity of the rumor that a volunteer had cheated on her husband with their valet parking attendant. Lily empathized with the middle Georgia team in New Bethel, as they vented about their local politicians taking credit for their efforts. Despite their disparate regions, they were all hungover and ready for the next stage in the battle. What was the plan?

Ford called the meeting to order, asking for everyone's patience as they squeezed into the small space. He paced back and forth in the front of the room, his hand covering his mouth, like he was preventing himself from revealing a secret too early. Perhaps they had finally received the full budget from Denver needed to win.

"Everyone, thank you for coming on such short notice. It is important that we all meet so we can begin the next phase of our plan to win. I know some of you are still working on building more volunteer teams, but we need to forge ahead." Lily thought he was looking right at her, but perhaps he meant the team from New Bethel who sat right behind her. She hadn't reached her goal of 20 volunteer teams yet, but the few she had could take on anyone's 20. Besides, she had told Ford numerous times that it takes time out there in the rural parts.

"Now it is time to motivate you, and my words are simply not enough to convey the motivation this crowd needs." Lily was relieved. She had softened towards Ford, but by no means was he Cady or Lowell Quarterman. Perhaps Rachel would say something. "What I'm about to show you is something you will then show to your teams all across the state. And this will be the fuel that fires their engines! Does anyone recall Henry the Fifth's epic battle with France?"

Uh oh.

"No. What's that?" someone shouted from the audience.

"Never heard of it."

"Me neither."

Lily sunk lower into her seat as Ford explained Medieval England. Rachel threw her lighter against the wall next to Ford. Angela rolled her eyes. The rest stared blankly, confused. *Please just don't show the movie.* Ford cut the lights and treated the crowd to a screening of a clip from the Kenneth Branagh version of *Henry V* where the king rallied the troops on the Feast Day of St. Crispin:

And gentlemen in England now a-bed
Shall think themselves accursed they were not here,
And hold their manhoods cheap whiles any speaks
That fought with us upon Saint Crispin's day.

"Can you rewind to the part where he says "England?"

"Who are they fighting again?"

"This is when England was at war with France in the year 1415. Morale was low. The French were mighty, but Henry V gave this speech to motivate his hungry and tired troops." Ford explained. He couldn't find an MLK speech? She would've settled for Churchill. "This clip is uploaded to our staff site, where you can show every one across Georgia this important speech."

She wondered how Ford was ever put in charge of Georgia. As if she had read her mind, Rachel texted her. "Dad runs big ad co. U heard of DeJeune & DeJeune?"

After the history lesson, Ford finally introduced the staff to the next phase of Georgia's field strategy, which contained three parts: (1) Inter-region competition, in which each region would be pitted against one another in a quest for metrics, goals, and volume; (2) Labor Day Extravaganza, a blowout weekend of voter registration a month away from the final deadline for voter registration, involving 72 hours of non-stop voter registration ("The biggest voter registration event in the history of democracy," Ford emphasized); and (3) The Peach State Reporting Tool (or "The Peach"). Ford signaled for Gianna to play introduction music. "I created this myself."

"Isn't this is a Google Doc app?" whispered Parker.

"Yeah, but with a Peach Icon," said Sam.

The Peach was where organizers would report their registration totals nightly. Then they would be compared to all the others in the field.

"Denver will be watching your results," concluded Ford. Lily was skeptical. For one, this was a self-reporting tool. How did they know who was reporting accurate numbers? And, more importantly, how can they have a winning strategy without increased funding for supplies or more staff? Instead, they had to produce more with the same resources and volunteers. Shame and competition were the tools for increased productivity.

Ford closed the meeting by naming the first regions to face off in the competition. Lily and North Georgia were to face off with the Middle Georgia region of New Bethel. She assessed the competition. New Bethel, led by Justin with the Cady logo dotting his "i", had five staffers; she had only three. But she had the best volunteers, those with battle wounds of a night in jail. And she now sported a Cady baseball cap.

After returning to the office, Lily introduced the intra-regional competition to an excited team in Ludlow. Elizabeth and Denise hatched plans to dominate the competition. Kent and Sarah couldn't wait to tell their son in Los Angeles of their next adventure. James hoped to get arrested again with his latest crush as witness. She gave everyone an individual goal of

50 registrations each day. The highest so far. But if they succeeded they would defeat New Bethel. Defeating New Bethel suddenly became paramount for the group. The intra-region competition actually worked.

"Bunch of rednecks there," said Denise.

"Yeah, and they're at least 3 hours off the interstate." Ken said. She didn't point out that Ludlow was almost 2 hours away. But whatever motivated the crew was what worked. On Saturday morning her Kitchen Cabinet and their latest recruits of new volunteers arrived promptly at 8 a.m. She sent them on their way with their turf packet and registration forms and, with confidence, they fanned out across the region.

CHAPTER 17

Lily spent the first morning canvassing an apartment complex located off Highway 16. She had noticed it every morning on her drive to the office, but had never stopped to take a look. The location hadn't been on any of the canvass maps generated by the VAN, but she needed to squeeze every possible registration out of the region. So she took a chance, parked her car in the visitor lot, and knocked on a door. She had been nervous, unsure whether she would be welcomed. But, much to her delight, wearing a Cady baseball hat was all that she needed. People greeted her like she was their long lost cousin. Children skipped behind her as she walked the stone path between apartments, peppering her with questions about Cady. Grandmothers gave her baked goods to take back to the office. Even when her car stalled due to a dead car battery, two teenagers not only jumped the battery but offered to inspect the engine for any other problems as well. In the three years she lived in her old Upper East Side apartment, she'd barely conversed this much with any of her neighbors. She was usually in a rush and gave the cursory *hello* in the mailroom and *thanks* if someone had held the elevator door open.

She quietly rejoiced in her triumph of 47 registrations. Her own registration along with Sam and Parker's totaled 50.

Georgia had only a 60-day residency requirement to vote. This was the one election law that pleased her. She sifted through the other registrations that had come in from the morning shift. Her reverie was interrupted by Elizabeth, who rushed inside with her arms flailing in the air, her handbag hitting her waist.

She had been assigned Banks County, a county smaller than Lily's law school's graduating class. She began to indulge Lily with the kind of rapid fire moment by moment detail usually reserved for crime fighting shows.

"I stopped at a gas station, just 6.2 miles off Highway 15. The air was cooler than usual for a typical Saturday in September. I had less than a quarter tank. They didn't have those credit swipes. So I went inside. Chatted with the gas station attendant. He noticed my Cady sticker." She paused for a breath. "He asked about it. I told him what I was doing. He confessed he was a supporter too, but not registered. He's from Sri Lanka and was naturalized over ten years ago and has yet to ever vote. Can you believe that? Of course I had to run out and register him."

Lily nodded in agreement.

"Two guys followed me back to the car. Probably the same age as Luke, but didn't look like Luke at all. Luke is much more handsome. One was chubby, with his stomach pouring over his jeans. The other, skinny as a pole, with a long beard that fell nearly to his chest. Well, the skinny one stood in front of the door, not letting me back into my car. *You can't come round these parts and do what you're doing,* he said. Can you believe that? The gall. Yes, I can, I said. I most certainly can. Then I scootched by him and started to get in the car. And, oh my, Lily, you won't believe it."

"What?" Ford had called twice during Elizabeth's story.

"The chubby one slammed the door on my hand."

"Oh, no." She rushed over to Elizabeth and carefully examined her hand. "Are you hurt?"

"I stopped him right before the door shut. And kicked him where it counted." Her eyes twinkled. "And then I punched the skinny one in the nose. He didn't know I was a lefty."

"Elizabeth, I don't know what to say. I'm so sorry this happened."

"I know I'm not supposed to use violence in response. It's against what I was taught, but I just couldn't help it," she admitted. "I'll have to confess," she continued sheepishly, "this was more fun than jail time, dear. Those two scampered away, especially after the attendant came out with a shotgun." She grabbed more registration forms, a couple of granola bars and a bottle of water.

"I'm headed further east now. See what I can get off Hwy. 11."

"You really don't need to go." But, she wanted her to. She needed her to meet the goal.

"Don't you worry. I will have those 50 by the time I get back."

Lily buried any worry about Elizabeth's safety. The most important thing was that every one got 50 registrations. Only Luke was concerned. He had stopped by the office to fix the printer connection, and she immediately regretted recounting the story.

"My mother went back out after that? I know she's tough. But she's been working all morning."

"We're neck and neck with New Bethel."

"Don't you find this a little over the top?"

No, she didn't. They had to win the state. And in order to win, they had to push their volunteers harder. Competition helped. This was a basic tenet in battle. Didn't Sun Tzu say this? She made a mental note to read the *Art of War*. Just as she was about to answer him, Denise rushed in with Kent and Sarah trailing a few steps behind her.

"What a morning! I thought jail was an adventure."

"How many registrations did you get?"

Denise pointed to Sarah.

"We decided to go to that Freedom Day Festival all the way out in Madison County."

"You mean a Labor Day Festival?"

"They called it Freedom Day." Of course they did.

"They let us set up a table behind the port-a-potties. After we posted the fliers and banners for people to register, two guys with German Shepherds parked their pick-up truck in front of the booth," Sarah explained.

"They hung a huge confederate flag on the tailgate." Denise interrupted. "Rednecks, I tell you."

"It was the old state flag that had the confederate logo." Kent corrected.

"When Kent wanted to use the bathroom," Sarah continued and took Kent's arm lovingly, "The dogs lurched toward him. Not letting him go." He lowered his head in shame. "We were even wearing matching bulldog hats with our shirts. The worst part about it was that not even one person stopped by to register." Lily couldn't hide her dismay.

"It's only 3 p.m. Let's see where else you can go." She printed out the canvass and call data sheets to pinpoint population density and found an apartment complex in which they could spend the rest of the afternoon. Luke quelled his disagreement and focused on the printer wires.

The rest of the day resulted in similar stories of intimidation. James got thrown in a dumpster. Someone tried to snatch Denise's handbag (Lily had told her to leave it at home). Sam's car ended up in a field after being chased by a motorcycle gang. By 9 p.m., Lily was extremely nervous as The Peach showed Middle Georgia had taken a sizable lead over North Georgia. This time when Ford called her, she anticipated his demands. "I know. We're going to push harder tomorrow."

"Do whatever it takes," he affirmed. "If we don't meet our goals this weekend, Wright will pull the plug on Georgia. But don't tell anyone else that. I just need you to understand." It was two months left until Election Day, and Cady could win 270 electoral votes without Georgia. He could win both Ohio and Florida. He probably didn't even need a southern state if he won those two states. But they had to win Georgia. They had to win for all the volunteers who were busting their asses and emptying their wallets to keep the effort alive. They had to win for all those at the People's Rally who rejoiced at the promise of tomorrow. They had to win for Lowell Quarterman who was running for county coroner. And they had to win, because Lamar Lovell began the work back in 1959 when he sat down at Randall's lunch counter and ordered a soda. She ordered everyone to report for an early morning meeting.

"It's Sunday. Church Day. We start later on those days." Parker reminded her.

"This *is* God's work. I'll also bring donuts."

The next morning, as they munched on pecan delights, Lily explained Georgia's precarious position as a battleground state. This immediately provoked a flurry of unanswerable questions.

"Does that mean Georgia is not winnable? Should I go help my cousin in North Carolina?" asked James.

"Will Cady still come here?" wondered Miss Louise.

"What happens to you?" asked Elizabeth. Lily was shocked by the question. She hadn't thought about her own situation.

"These questions are pointless, because we are going to win. Now, I told you all of this so that you would understand how important today and tomorrow are. Are you guys willing to work harder?" They all cheered in unison. "Yes!" They decided this time they would go to various fast food chains and register customers, hoping the managers didn't interfere. Lily wouldn't even try asking for permission in advance. Parker heard from her friend on Team Augusta that they were having tremendous success going to apartment complexes that were not in the VAN.

"I got 47 from one of them. Yes let's do it," ordered Lily.

She had made the right decision in revealing the stakes. That evening she tallied up the results and reported them into The Peach which now showed them tied with Middle Georgia, with only one day left in the competition. It was nearly 10 p.m., and she and Sam pored through the registrations, doublechecking that the driver's license numbers and addresses were correctly reported.

The door chimed opened and she could now smell Larry from a block away.

"Larry, I think the liquor store is closed."

"Oh, yes, ma'am." But instead of turning around, he came inside.

"It's closed." She repeated.

"Yes mam. I know. I wanted to give you these." He handed her three rumpled registration forms. She opened them up, and sure enough one was for Larry, and the other two were from the liquor store managers. They had the lead.

"Larry, this is wonderful! Thank you." She hugged him tightly and kissed him on the cheek. Sam hugged him as well. "Want a drink?" She took the whiskey off the shelf and the three of them sipped from paper cups, while Larry told them of the time he spent in Bangkok during the Vietnam War.

"This office, well what it used to look like before y'all got here, kinda looks like this bar I used to frequent. It had duct tape holding its windows together too."

"I've never been," said Lily.

"Me neither." Sam said.

"Gracious. Never been anywhere so gracious." Larry filled his cup to the brim. He began to chuckle to himself.

"What is it?" asked Sam.

"Just thinking of that time I got all of those dockworkers to do a kick-line on the bar, singing New York, New York. They wore those yellow rubber boots that went all the way up to your knees. And they were so short that from the table all you could see was this bright streak of yellow soles across that dingy bar. Like a ray of rubber sunshine." He refilled the cup, again. "I try not to remember too much from that time. But I do like to remember that."

Lily stood up on her desk and reached her arm out to Larry. "C'mon up." She grabbed Sam's arm too. And the three of them pounded on the desk singing New York, New York, while the bald eagle lamp remained intact.

Later, after they had finished the bottle, and Larry had stumbled off toward his apartment, Lily locked up and the two of them returned to entering the registrations into the database.

"Where's Parker?" asked Sam, weary-eyed from deciphering handwriting.

Lily shrugged. "I don't know. Maybe she stopped to get something to eat?"

"No, she would call me to grab dinner."

"Then, I don't know. We've got to get through all these registrations and it's not like I'm her babysitter. She's *your* girlfriend." She didn't want to be snappish, but she was drunk and tired. They had until midnight to process all the registrations for the day.

"I'm worried," Sam said. "She wanted to hit up this apartment complex she stumbled onto that wasn't on our list. I told her it was too late to go, and that I would go with her tomorrow, but she insisted." Lily smiled to herself. That girl had gusto. Depending on how many more registrations Parker got, they could have a clear advantage over Middle Georgia going into the last day of competition. Both Sam and Parker had changed since that first day she met them. They slept more nights in their supporter housing in Ludlow than in their Buckhead apartment. They often stayed at the office later than Lily, entering the last amount of data or printing call sheets for the next day. They didn't have nearly as much sex.

"Well, then call her," suggested Lily.

"I've tried, but it keeps going to voice mail. Probably out of range. This whole damn region is out of range."

"Oh, she's fine." She would be. If it was anything like her own experience yesterday, Parker probably stayed to eat dinner with some locals. "But, let's keep trying." They alternated calling Parker and reviewing registrations, until past midnight. Sam was on the verge of filing a missing persons report, when Parker's Mini-Cooper, driven by Representative Winslow, rolled onto the gravel lot. A moment later a police car drove up beside it. Winslow and Day hurried toward the office, with the policeman trailing behind. Lily suddenly felt guilty for dismissing Sam's concerns. What on earth were they doing with Parker's car? Sam rushed to unlock the door.

"Miss Day-Marco, we have a problem," Winslow announced. It was the first time she'd seen him without a suit.

"Yes?" Lily stood up from the behind the desk.

"What's wrong? Where's Parker?" Sam asked.

"She's at County Hospital. She's been shot," Day replied. The officer nodded.

"Wait, what? What are you saying?" Sam yelled. Lily slumped back into her chair.

Winslow leaned across her desk, his face squarely in front of hers. "This is the South. Like I said to you, we have different rules. She can't go waltzing into certain neighborhoods with that fancy car of hers and a bunch of Cady signs and think she'll be welcomed." He couldn't hide his scorn. "That's what I'm here for."

CHAPTER 18

Lily sank into bed after spending the early morning hours at the hospital. Thankfully the novice shooter had poor aim and only grazed Parker's arm. She would recover in a couple of days and return to work. But why would she want to? Lily let this ridiculous competition get the best of her. She should never have pushed her staff so hard. Sam was pissed at her. Parker was in shock. Ford wanted a plan to achieve their goals without Parker's involvement. And Lily didn't want to get out of bed. Not later this morning. Not ever. The campaign would go on without her. She would cast an absentee ballot for Cady in Georgia and call it a day. She just wasn't cut out for this. Working out of a shack with dial-up internet, swatting gnats half the day, eating fried pickles and pickles baked in cheese. Battling Ford. Battling Denver. Battling Winslow. Forcing her volunteers to do more with increasingly less. She didn't have Denise's boldness or Miss Louise's grit. She didn't have Elizabeth's heart or Sarah and Ken's love. She didn't even have Luke's indifference. She was done.

She called Gabe. "Do you need help on the farm?"

"Really? You've been so engrossed down there with the campaign. It takes you at least 24 hours to respond to my text. You want to leave?"

"I think the campaign has brought out the worst in me."

"Well, you care about what you're doing. That's probably why. I cried when the summer squash got infected by pests. Ruined the whole vine. Then, I spent the week watching Seasons 1 and 2 of Ex-Housewives of Beverly Hills. Watching them interview for their first jobs was therapeutic."

"How do I say goodbye to everyone? It's not like leaving Heels & Ellsworth. I want to stay in touch with them. I want to know what Mrs. Louise's real name is. I want to know if James ends up asking his new crush to prom. Or if Sarah and Kent secure a better tailgating spot away from the Republicans."

"Tailgating? Are you already drinking?"

She considered having a bloody mary this morning.

"It's hard to leave. Much harder than I thought."

"It always is. Just know there's a space for you on the farm. On the other side of the house. Away from the chickens. It's just like on TV. Those roosters really do cuckoo early in the morning. "

"I love you, Gabe."

"Love you more."

She searched the house for Elizabeth to let her know how much she appreciated sharing her home with her and how sad she was to be leaving, but instead she found Luke in the garage. He took the news surprisingly well. "Sure. I get it. This isn't your home and where you want to be. So of course the job is too much." He was rummaging through old tools and equipment in the garage. Separating them into two piles. Useful and dated. She was dated. Just like that old DSL router he had tossed into the pile. Her life plans constantly muted and interrupted by static. "Since you've got a little more time on your hands now, want to join?" He asked. He held the power drill in one hand and the toolbox in the other.

"Sure." She responded. "Where are we going?"

"The office. I'm finally putting in a brand new window."

"Just as I'm leaving."

"See what you'll miss."

The office was empty that morning. After Parker's incident, Ford allowed her to give the volunteers the day off. Yet they refused and planned on reconvening by lunch. She would have to figure out what to say when they arrived. She hadn't told Ford about her plans to leave. She hadn't told anyone other than Luke. It was easier to tell him. They began working on the window by wrestling the old boards out of the wall.

"So why did you really leave Chicago?" She asked. Now that she was leaving, she wanted to know Luke's real story.

He paused for a moment and then continued to tug at the boards.

"I thought I told you. My mom needed help."

"Luke, your mom is the least helpless person I know."

He smiled. He then set the old boards and picked up the new frame.

"It's a long story. Messy."

She glanced at the clock. "We've got at least two hours before everyone gets here."

This time he laughed. "I guess it's short and messy."

"So what happened? Chicago to Ludlow?"

He began to nail the frame. "I moved to Chicago after college. Didn't really know anyone until I started working. Became good buddies with this guy Jeff. He worked at the same architecture firm as me."

He hesitated and surveyed her, as if he was unsure whether to continue. She nodded in encouragement. He continued nailing.

"I became close friends with his girlfriend, too. Anna Lise. She was also a lawyer, by the way." He studied her for a second and then continued. "At the time our friendship ... well, it became more than that." He paused. "I ended up falling for her." His voice trailed off.

"Oh, wow," she said. "What happened?"

"I don't know if I should say anymore. You're going to think the worst of me."

"It's ok. I won't. We all make mistakes."

"That's the thing, I didn't think it was a mistake at the time. We were going to tell Jeff. She was going to leave him. I was going to ask her to marry me. And then she did tell Jeff about us … and…" He put down the hammer and slumped to the floor. His back was against the wall. He turned his face away from Lily's.

"And?"

"She didn't leave him."

She slowly sat down beside him; her shoulders gently touching his arms. They sat quietly. She didn't think any less of him. She wanted to cradle him in her arms. The pain of losing both a friend and a love at exactly the same time was something she never wanted to experience.

"I was fired."

He looked up. "You mean the campaign—?"

"No. I was fired from my last job. I didn't bill enough hours. I had tried to, but things just didn't work out."

"I'm sorry."

"It was the worst feeling. No matter how hard I tried, I still didn't measure up."

"I know that feeling."

"And then to end up back in my parents' basement. That's where I was before I came here."

He laughed.

"What's so funny?"

"I'm living above my mom's garage."

She laughed along with him. Then they both grew silent again. He took her hand.

"You were right, Luke. This wasn't my first choice to come here. This was a Plan B. But now, it's become more than that. It's more than just a plan."

He smiled and started playing with her fingers.

"Chicago just didn't work out. Besides, I prefer a smaller, quieter place. I like it here. I know it sounds stupid. A small town like this. And maybe at some point I may move closer to Atlanta, but right now this is good."

She surveyed the tiny campaign office that had become her second home. Denise's bright pillows poked through the piles of canvass and call sheets. James's electric guitar, with which he serenaded the office with his latest jazz/rock composition, rested by its amplifier. A roll of Dawgs for Cady stickers, created by Sarah and Ken, lay unfurled on a desk salvaged from Miss Louise's yard sale. Luke's tools lay beside her. She held his hand. "Yes, this is good."

He squeezed her hand gently, but firmly. They sat in silence for a moment longer, holding hands and listening to the hum of the air conditioner. She wanted to hold his hand for as long as she could. But there was work to be done. He finished nailing the new window frame, while she began to straighten up the rest of the office. She papered the walls with the campaign posters, letters, and pictures from supporters that had piled up over the months. The two of them then taped the hundred Cady pledge cards, collected by a local barbecue restaurant, right by the doorway. It was nearly noon and the team would arrive in an hour. She couldn't wait for everyone to see the spruced up office and the new window.

And she knew at that moment that she couldn't leave. She was going to stick it out no matter how many grazed bullets her staff endured.

"Want to grab a burger before the others get here?" he asked as he packed the tools in a box.

"Only if it's got pimento cheese."

"What else is there?"

CHAPTER 19

Georgia surpassed its registration goals and beat all the other battleground states in the number of voters registered. "Georgia will be on top of all the other states' reports when Cady reviews the campaign operations this weekend," Ford announced. Lily and the volunteers crowded around the speaker of her Blackberry.

"Maybe now we will get a real speakerphone," Lily muttered. Good thing she was on mute.

"Now as a special surprise, Wright from Denver is on the call."

Denise stood up at attention. "This guy is a genius. Did you know he barely graduated from college? Genius I tell you."

After witnessing Ford grovel with Wright for resources, Lily had grown weary of Wright's campaign talk. While he never outright said any new resources were coming, he kept dangling that possibility. In return, Ford would just push everyone to work harder. They were like rabbits jumping higher for a carrot only for it to be pulled even higher by its master. Still she listened attentively along with the others.

"Georgia, you fucking rock. You did an amazing job this weekend. It's just fucking shocking what you did." Sarah's pale white face turned red.

"But I know you're tired of hearing from me all the time. So, I've got someone I know you want to hear from. Governor, are you there?"

The room erupted. Some quickly brushed their hair and touched up makeup as if Cady was about to walk right into the room. Others began to shush them, not wanting to miss a single moment. Lily turned up her Blackberry speaker volume as loud as it could go. "Do we have a microphone?" asked James. She shook her head in response. She placed her Blackberry in the center of the room, elevated on a chair. They all huddled close around it.

"Well, hello Georgia!" The room squealed. Some threw air punches and karate kicks.

"You guys had an amazing weekend, and I just want to thank you for what you have done. Not only have you made a difference to this campaign, but you've shown what this campaign was all about. I said from the beginning this was a bottom up campaign, and you've certainly demonstrated that. Your efforts have brought more people to the political process than at any time since the abolishment of the Jim Crow laws. And that is simply remarkable. Thank you, and let's keep up the hard work. We still have a lot to do."

They rejoiced. Hugs and tears. "He's coming down here. I just know it. He's coming!" shouted Miss Louise.

"We are actually going to win here," said Elizabeth. "Oh, my. After 40 years of living down here in Georgia. Never did I ever think."

"We'll probably get a copier. Don't you think?" Denise asked.

"Yes. I think we finally will," Lily replied. Her skepticism of Wright faded. Their struggle was finally being recognized. And not just with a congratulatory speech. Now that Georgia beat out all the other battlegrounds states with a shoestring budget, the campaign would have to put some resources into the effort. When they did, victory would be inevitable. She began to salivate at how efficiently they could work with a copy machine. She could distribute four times as many canvass and call packets in a two hour shift. They decided to celebrate at the local diner with pimento cheese brulée and unknown quantities of sparkling wine. Everyone reminisced of their jail time, recounted their flirtations with danger, and reveled in their accomplishment. Later that night, after the revelry was over, she snuggled into bed and called Gabe. She left him a voice mail.

"No need to make up that spare bedroom. I'm staying. We're finally winning."

CHAPTER 20

Lily gathered Sam and Parker for yet another conference call, which Ford had announced late the night before. This time he specifically requested that only staff be on the call. No volunteers. They took the few moments before the call to review the latest news clips. She rarely read a full article in the paper anymore. Just web clips from the scroll feature of her Blackberry. And that was only when her car was stopped at a red light.

"Who is Ginnifer Rollins?" Parker asked. She was on her fifth day of prescribed pain killers. She sat in the metal folding chair like it was an easy-sleep mattress. Her polo shirt fell around her hips, untucked.

"Eaves's VP nominee," Lily responded. That morning Eaves had officially introduced Ginnifer Rollins as his Vice-Presidential running mate. Every newspaper and news channel led the morning news with that announcement.

"Yes, but who was she before that?"

"Lieutenant Governor of South Dakota," answered Sam.

"Who's the Governor?"

None of them had any idea. According to the papers, Rollins was a virtually unknown politician in many circles, even among the leaders of her own party.

Ford opened the call with another congratulations to the staff for their registration accomplishments and their outstanding Labor Day weekend success. "I'd like to now patch in Davis Wright, the boy wonder behind the campaign, who has devoted an entire 15 minutes this morning to talk to you, Georgia, and only you." Wright was just on the call two days ago. Why would he bother to get on again?

"I bet we're getting a raise!" Parker exclaimed.

"You should definitely ask for hazard pay," Lily replied.

"Hello, Team Georgia. Let me begin by telling you that everyone in Denver is talking about you and the work you have done down here in Georgia. Cady opened the morning yesterday looking at the numbers from Georgia. He could not be prouder of what you have accomplished down there in the 'Dirty South,' nor could we. You have managed to register far more voters than any other state; this Labor Day alone you registered 30,000 more voters than the closest state. You have by far the largest number of volunteers of any of our battleground states. You have built the strongest neighborhood teams. The work you have accomplished here will already go down in the history books. It is truly incredible. The good news is that the organization you have built here is so successful that we no longer need as many of you to be in Georgia to keep it running. We are going to move a portion of you to other states such as Ohio and Florida where the campaign needs help. We need for you to take the skills you have learned in Georgia and teach organizers and volunteers in these states where we are not polling the way we believe that we should be polling. Some of you will stay here to keep the campaign that all of you have so masterfully built running.

"Our decision to reallocate you, the resource of our staff, in no way reflects a belief that we no longer feel Georgia is winnable. You have proven just the opposite. It does not mean that we do not care about Georgia. Georgia has built a system of volunteers that rivals California in its level of self-sufficiency. We are not pulling out of Georgia. We are leaving a core group behind to manage this massive campaign of volunteers: a true grassroots campaign! It is important that you neither view this as abandoning Georgia nor pulling out of Georgia. It is equally important that this is not the message you deliver to the volunteers, the public, or the press. You control the way this message is being delivered, and if it is wrongly delivered, you risk hurting what you have so carefully and lovingly built. Ford and Gianna will let each of you know over the next week where you have been assigned. You should let your RFD know today whether your preference is to stay here or to go help in a state where we truly need the extra support and your expertise. I want to thank you on behalf of Governor Cady, and all of us in Denver and across the country, for what you have done here."

Parker laid her head on Sam's shoulder.

"It's just like the primaries. Here one day, gone the next," said Sam.

"I'm tired of moving around. Of living out of a suitcase."

"I know." He kissed her on the forehead.

Lily was silent. Leave Georgia? She just got here. She just installed a new window. Painted the walls. Alphabetized the pledge cards. She actually liked pimento cheese sandwiches. She hadn't fired the shotgun yet.

She was not leaving. She just made the decision to stay no matter what, and now the campaign may move her out. They were number one, damn it. Ohio and Florida screwed everyone once again. The sun, now higher in the sky, cast a brighter glare through the window next to the folding card table where they sat.

CHAPTER 21

The Atlanta headquarters was bare. Not a volunteer in sight. The laptops that usually lined the tables were gone. The tables were gone. Boxes of documents stood in lines at the shredder. Gone were the hand painted posters and colorful scribbling of Cady's slogans. No more bumper stickers or t-shirts. Only one old desktop computer remained in the reception area, flickering with past images of smiling volunteers with a display title "Hope Arrives." Only one Cady poster remained, listing from the wall on one nail. If she'd only known that three months ago the office was at its peak, she would've snapped a photo of it. She could hear her sneakers squeak against the linoleum. Three days had passed since she called to let Ford know that she, Sam, and Parker wanted to be the few who remained in Georgia. She heard nothing. She had called Rachel, too. No response. There were a few staffers who lingered in the office cleaning and packing. She found Angela and Tim packaging computer equipment. Angela looked visibly upset. Her eyelids were puffy, the under-eyes darker.

"Hey, Lily. Gianna has planned a going away party for the staff. You game?" asked Tim.

"But who's leaving? Who's staying?"

"I don't know. I do know D.Y. and Row Boy may be there." Tim's eyes narrowed. "Numbers 1 and 2 on the Rap 100 list."

Angela said nothing. Instead, she revealed a dejected look. She had never seen Angela so disheartened.

Lily still didn't know who they were, but pretended to play along. "I'll be sure to dust off my mini skirt for that one," Lily jibed. Angela cracked a smile in response.

She followed the smell of cigarette smoke back to Rachel's office.

"Fuck me in the armpits. Fuck me in my fucking armpits," said Rachel. Lily shut the door behind her.

"What's going on?"

"Wright has asked for at least two-thirds of the staff to be transferred. Ford and Gianna have been redoing the list of reassignments daily, turning it in only to redo it. Either Wright wants more people to go or he isn't happy with who's staying. It changes every round. Last I heard, you are headed to Florida and they want me in Indiana. Ford's going to Ohio, I think. It's all a disaster." Rachel quickly wiped her eyes. "I've heard some staff talk about quitting the official campaign so that they can stay and work in Georgia. I might do that. I might."

"I don't want to leave either. But quitting the campaign outright? I never thought it would come to this." She was torn. She wanted Cady to win. But she wanted Georgia to be part of that victory.

"I don't know what to do. I'm in unknown territory." Rachel tried to light another cigarette, but the flame kept fluttering. It wouldn't catch. She tossed the lighter aside and slumped back into her chair.

"Lily," Ford peeked his door into the office. "I heard you were here. Can we talk?"

She followed him down the hall. "You've got to convince Wright to let us stay. Convince him we can win this state. The numbers are there. We've registered over 100,000 people so far."

He studied her for a moment. "I'm glad you came down to Atlanta. Do you mind giving me a ride back to my housing?"

"These teams have done — no wait, are doing — an amazing job. But they still need us here. We can't just leave them. We are so close." They climbed into her car. She tossed her empty Chick N'Bik wrappers into the back seat.

"Gianna really wants me to be at this party tonight and I'm beat. Every night it's one event after another. Just once I want to relax in my suite with a bottle of Bordeaux and watch West Wing reruns." He rested his head against the passenger side window and closed his eyes.

"You have a suite?"

"I know. I have to court the high donors. But, how many Alizé cocktails can one drink?" He muttered.

"Ford, what is going on?" He woke up and sat upright in the seat.

"Frankly, it's all a mess. Wright's demands keep going up. He first wanted to leave two thirds of staff in the state; now it's down to one quarter: a true skeleton. I'll maybe end up leaving four staffers. I think we've finally come to an agreement."

"Only four? How can we get anything done?"

"You've got all the volunteer teams across the state."

"You've got to insist with Denver. Push harder. Ask for more people."

"I'll know for certain in the morning."

"Where am I taking you?"

"Go north four blocks and turn right on 14th Street. I actually have asked Wright for you to stay and run the state with Rachel running data and Tim and Angela staying with Atlanta."

"Wait. Me? No, I can't run this thing. I want to stay here, but put Rachel in charge."

"Do you see that hotel on the left? You can turn in there." She pulled into a large white post-modern tower with a well-heeled crowd waiting outside along a velvet rope to enter the hotel's bar.

"The W?"

"Yes, please."

"I thought I was taking you home?"

"I actually live here."

"This is the supporter housing that connected you with the neighborhood?"

"It was the most convenient place to the office, and considering I don't have a car ..."

They sat silently for a moment in her car parked just beyond the valet's reach.

"It is not going to be easy. The Persuasion phase is essentially out. Leave it to the media buys. Just focus on getting every one of the registrants to vote. And then some. Rachel is a whiz at targeting. She'll find those voters." He gazed at her with empathy.

"Why me? I don't understand."

His voice then grew softer. "I didn't think you would be able to do anything out there in Ludlow. Honestly, I put you out there because you hadn't worked in the primary and figured that was the least priority section of the state. I figured anything you did was just icing on the cake."

"I knew it!" She impulsively punched his shoulder.

"Oww."

"You deserve it."

"Lily, Wright wanted you in Florida. I made the case for you to stay here. What you did out in Ludlow with absolutely nothing is freaking outstanding. Sure, I gave you high registration goals, but honestly, I didn't think you would even get a tenth of it. Your region is over halfway to their goals. It's truly remarkable. Which is why you're the perfect person to be in charge."

"But I want to stay in Ludlow." She surprised herself with those words.

"You can't. The four of you need to be in Atlanta."

"What about Parker and Sam?"

"Parker is slated for Florida and Sam is off to Ohio. I haven't told Rachel yet. Waiting on confirmation from Wright."

"She's probably going to quit if she doesn't stay."

"Georgia's all yours now. Good luck." He scampered off into the hotel. She felt like a child who had just been given a broken toy.

She found Rachel at the office with a pack of unopened cigarettes and a full bottle of whiskey. Her books were strewn on the floor.

"I can't drink. I can't smoke. Something is really wrong with me. Maybe I need to go to the hospital." A vegan cookie lay uneaten on her desk.

"Just inhale once and see how you feel."

"My ex was right. I wasn't happy with him because it was real. Instead, I spend my time in fantasy land. One cause to another. One state to the next. I felt more alive going than staying. Until now. God, I'm 32. Did you know? Thirty fucking two. Do yourself a favor Lily. Go back to New York." Rachel slumped back into her desk chair and flicked her lighter on and off. Lily would be 31 in December. She pulled up a chair next to Rachel and poured them both a drink. She waited until Rachel took a sip. And then she did as well. They listened to the creaks and hums of an empty office.

"Lily? Lily, are you back there?" She recognized the voice immediately, closed the door behind her and ran out into the hallway.

"Gabe, what are you doing here?" She hugged him tightly, refusing to let go.

"With this welcome, I should've come earlier!" he said. He had let his straight dark hair grow out to almost chin length, and it shined of the latest product. He wore close fitting jeans, sneakers, and loose grey sweatshirt, which was one size too big for him.

She pulled two folding chairs together and they sat down. He looked around the stark office. "It looks almost like Buffalo Steers, except we still had AC."

"Did you just get here? Why? How long can you stay?" Lily hoped until November.

"After your texts and emails and then your last voice mail, I had to come see everything for myself. I only get calls or emails for money. I had to see what was happening on the ground. I had to see you making it happen."

"I can't believe you are here!"

"I can only stay a couple of days. Got a last minute cheap fare. Fall harvest starts soon. Here's a check from Rick. He's worried you don't have money for groceries. And Rita sewed a sweater for that bald eagle. Lamp, huh? I love Rita."

"He's such a worrier. You won't believe how much Elizabeth cooks. And the volunteers, well, I could pretty much open up a bakery with the amount of goodies they bring in." She hugged him again. She could smell the earthy scent of fertile soil. He was still lean but she felt the strength of his muscles by his embrace. Farm living suited him. She didn't want to let go.

"Tell me about your man, Cady, the campaign. Have you met Cady? Oh my god, and Eaves's VP pick. I was never a big fan of beauty queens. I can tolerate a state pageant, though, but inside the Oval Office?

"Well, I wouldn't say Luke is my man."

"Not yet."

"And the campaign is moving some people out of Georgia. But thankfully, I'm staying. We have two months left. And we can win this thing."

"What are you talking about? The Times, Journal, and every other paper reported Cady pulled out of Georgia. He's going to win this election. He doesn't need Georgia."

"Well, sure, they moved most of the staff." She couldn't reveal that it was everyone but four. "But they left me here. Left me in charge."

"You're boss lady?! That's great, Lily, it really is. I get it. Even when I knew Buffalo Steers was on its last breath, I didn't want to leave until they actually shut the building down."

"We can win this, Gabe. I really think we can. You've got to see our office in Ludlow. It's so charming now. And, you've got to meet all the volunteers. Now, when you meet Luke, do not tell him I told you about our kiss. You can sleep on Elizabeth's couch. I've told her all about you. And, we'll have to eat at Chick N' Bik of course. Did you know that tangy sauce is pimento cheese? They put pimento on everything down here. "

"I've never seen you so excited. So alive. Really, Lil, you look beautiful."

She realized she'd been wearing the same t-shirt from yesterday and her jeans had flecks of chocolate icing from the morning donuts and traces of the Chick N' Bik cheese sauce from yesterday's lunch. Her hair was frizzier than usual.

"Look at us," she said. "We used to wear suits and drink cocktails at the hotel bar. Now you're on a farm. And I'm in a field office in Georgia."

"Two modern day pioneers." He snapped a photo of the two of them with his phone.

She laughed. "For once, I have no idea what I'm doing. I have no idea how tomorrow will turn out."

"I know. Doesn't it feel great?" he asked.

She hugged him tighter.

CHAPTER 22

Was it the baggy t-shirt that made her hips look bigger? No. She was chubby. Three months of fast food drive-thrus and a potpourri of fried food had left her plump and greasy. She looked like Georgia. She had last plucked her eyebrows in the South Carolina motel room before her first night on the campaign. Now she looked worse than the 55 year-old attendant who had smoked cloves behind the front desk. She missed Gabe already, even though he had only left the day before. She had given him the whirlwind tour of Ludlow and her volunteers before saying goodbye to him. And now she had to say goodbye to Ludlow. She slowly packed her room, gathering the t-shirts and shorts strewn around. She made sure to place Lovell's memoir in her backpack to return to Rachel. The three days in limbo awaiting Denver's orders had provided her with just enough time to finish reading it. While the requisite American History classes in high school and college had taught her about the policies, laws, and the leaders of the civil rights movement, the memoir revealed to her the day-to-day struggle of the people who worked on the ground in the south. It was unlike anything anyone experienced elsewhere. Not only were they battling other people and institutions, but they were also always fighting for resources from the national organizations based in D.C. or New York. What Lovell and his group had accomplished on principle and hands-on work was inspiring, the rare kind of story that never made it to a two minute television spot, but could only be understood by reading it cover to cover. She felt guilty about pestering Ford for an AC unit, and she vowed no longer to complain about the Georgia heat.

The smell of Elizabeth's French toast wafted through the house. That first breakfast three months ago seemed like three years ago.

"I've made some cheese grits along with the French toast. You're probably addicted by now." Elizabeth said.

"Yes, I guess I am." She would miss Elizabeth and her home away from home. Later that day she would move into the Buckhead apartment vacated by Sam and Parker and which Parker's father had paid up until November. It was gated and had a gym, not that she would ever get the chance to use it. She wondered if they served cheese grits, the creamy kind with butter and real cheddar, in Buckhead?

"We will miss you here. All of us," Elizabeth said. "I know Atlanta is only a couple of hours' drive, but for us that feels like New York."

"I'm just happy they didn't move me to Florida or Ohio." Although, now the full endeavor of running the entire state's operations with four staffers was beginning to sink in. Why did she agree to let Ford put her in charge? At times she barely kept it together out here in Ludlow. She mulled over these unanswerable questions.

"I just can't believe he picked a beauty queen college dropout." Elizabeth muttered, referencing the Eaves Vice-Presidential pick. "There were so many better choices in his own party. Women who know the difference between Iraq and Iran and read the newspaper every day."

She swirled the maple syrup into a circle on her plate, listening to Elizabeth as she continued her rant about the possibility of a Rollins Vice-Presidency actually reversing women's advancement.

"She did eventually graduate," Lily offered.

"He could've picked Senator White from New Hampshire or Governor Talley of Tennessee. But no. He's got no clue about women. No one wants to be replaced by someone younger, prettier, and inexperienced."

"Well, choosing her did do the trick." Eaves's poll numbers were up after the Rollins pick. They were up higher in Georgia than in the other battleground states. This was probably the impetus for Wright to move 90 percent of the staff out of here, leaving her high and dry and alone with just Angela, Rachel, and Tim. She had to leave Denise, Miss Louise, Elizabeth, Kent, Sarah, and James. Grooming at SaveAlot had grown on her. Now she'd have to find a real salon, one that served tea while she waited. The only things she wouldn't miss were her run-ins with Winslow and Day.

"Good morning, dear. Breakfast?" Elizabeth greeted Luke. He poured a coffee into a thermos.

"Can't. Need to run." He kissed his mother on the cheek and then paused at Lily.

"Sorry to see you leave Ludlow." He said it as if he expected it all along.

"It's only Atlanta. Just an hour and a half drive. I've made it there and back on a half of a tank of gas. With your truck, maybe it will take an entire tank, but it's still pretty close. And I'm on the north end of the city, so closer to Ludlow than the south side which is closer to the airport, but you know that already." She bit her lip to prevent any more rambling.

"I'll give you a call if I make it down that way," he said and gave her a pat on the back like the family pet.

She watched him stroll out the front door and heard the screen door slam shut behind him. They hadn't had a moment alone since that morning when they fixed the broken window and when he told her about his real reason for leaving Chicago. She wondered if this was the end. Not that anything had ever really begun. She might as well go to Atlanta. She could at least return to sushi. Maybe she'd finally lose the 11 pounds she gained.

"I know everyone is waiting at the office to say goodbye. We are definitely going to miss you here," said Elizabeth.

"I'm going to miss y'all too."

"You said y'all!"

"Holy crap. I did."

"Took me 2 years. It only took you three months. Georgia suits you."

The same sentiments were repeated at the office. Kent and Sarah shed tears and James gave her a framed copy of his mug shot. "My life is way more interesting because of you."

Miss Louise handed her the shotgun from the closet. "Just in case, dear."

"No. I'll be in Atlanta. You need it here."

"Please take it with you. It'll make me feel better."

Denise explained that she would be driving to Atlanta once a week to claim supplies for the office.

"What do you mean?" asked Lily.

"We're going to keep this place running," said Denise. "We've come up with a weekly schedule. James will open the office after school. Kent and Sarah offered to come after work and keep the office open late, since they need their Saturdays off for the football games." Kent and Sarah smiled sheepishly.

Denise continued. "I'll be here during the mornings on Tuesdays and Thursdays. Miss Louise will cover Monday, Wednesday, and Friday. Elizabeth will cover Saturday. And we are all here on Sunday after church. We'll raise money to operate it by printing some gray market t-shirts with Miss Louise's t-shirt press. " Miss Louise beamed at the thought. "We're going to keep this campaign office open regardless of Denver. Fuck Denver!"

"Yeah. Screw Denver!" Kent and Sarah's matching Bulldog t-shirts had evolved into matching fall sweatshirts.

"I can't believe it." Lily gazed at her little army she had cobbled together only three months ago. A motley crew that now had color coded charts for phone and canvass shifts, homemade t-shirts and bumper stickers for sale, and walk sheets printed with Google maps. They didn't need her at all. It nearly made her nostalgic for the early days when they did.

"You've organized yourself out of a job," Elizabeth whispered as she squeezed her shoulders.

"I'm really going to miss y'all," she said, and hugged everyone goodbye. Then she left the Ludlow office holding the shotgun erect and cradling the bald eagle lamp under her arm.

CHAPTER 23

She found Rachel smoking at her desk. The floor fan, although on high, barely made a dent in the haze. Lily had settled into Ford's old office across the hall. Angela and Tim kept their offices next to each other and closer to the reception area. The two of them were busy trying to scrounge up card tables and donated computer equipment from the volunteers they had organized in Atlanta. Phase II, which would have been persuasion — convincing independent voters that Cady's platform for universal health care, ending the war, and a green energy policy would offer America a better future than Eaves's platform — was eliminated. They were back to Phase I, securing donated supplies and keeping their volunteers organized.

"Smoking indoors?"

"Don't grow into a Gianna." She opened a new box of vegan cookies. "I'm craving a hotdog. Tim had barbecue rib sauce dripping down his cheek and I was tempted to lick."

"He probably would've enjoyed that."

"If he could only get those models to make 50 phone calls instead of clean his office."

She was relieved to have Rachel back again.

"He never scores, does he?"

"But he never stops trying."

"So how do we orchestrate the most impossible upset in political history?" Rachel asked.

"Maybe we start by yelling at Denver for more paper?"

"This is going to be fun."

Rachel's enthusiasm was contagious. There were only 60 days left to the election. Other than the Atlanta office, the rest of 11 statewide offices were without internet and phones, and essentially out of staff. Yet, she couldn't imagine being anywhere else.

A quick call from Alex in Davis Wright's office revealed that the new budget had yet to be approved. As if an old budget had ever been approved. She was no dummy. With awareness comes acceptance, right? They had accomplished more than any other state with the small amount that they had. They would figure out a way to keep going. She and Rachel began to brainstorm about ways to keep the volunteers motivated.

"How about a vegan bake-off?" Rachel suggested.

Lily searched for a tactfully crafted rejection, but was saved by Tim and Angela's fighting.

"She's out of control. She just threw away my stickers." Tim ran into Rachel's office with Angela at his heels.

"I didn't throw them away. I stole them. It's all we've got left, and I'm going to hand them out when I register tonight. You've been pimping them out to your models." Tim looked as if he was going to smack Angela. This was the beginning of their demise. A fierce squabble over a couple hundred campaign stickers, the last remaining resource this office had. If this was any indication of what the end of the world would resemble, it wasn't pretty.

"You're still going out to register?" Lily was unsure how to steer this slowly sinking ship.

"Of course. Why wouldn't we? We have 30 more days."

"But the campaign has left. We're not getting any more resources. I don't even know if we will still get paid. Maybe it's wise to focus our efforts on phone calling. I don't know if we have the manpower to keep canvassing and registering." She wanted to remain in Georgia, but the futility of their effort was slowly sinking in.

Angela stared at Lily in wonderment, like Lily was from a different generation — one of latch-key kids and skeptics.

"Why wouldn't we? We're still here." She flailed her arms at the four of them in the room. "And so are thousands of volunteers. Most of them are running the offices themselves."

"Yeah, but how long is that going to last?" Tim butted in. He flashed Lily a smile of solidarity. She did not want to choose his side of any disagreement.

"As long as they still think we care," Angela snapped back. She squeezed the last roll of stickers tightly, as if she was contemplating wrapping it around his neck.

"She's right," said Lily. "Even in my region, an islet of blue in a sea of red, my volunteers plan on running those offices until E-Day." What she would say next would pretty much eviscerate any chance of a lingering dinner. "We will operate the way we have been." Rachel and Angela nodded.

Tim smiled. "I like what we've been doing all along."

"Let's try and scrape up whatever resources we can. Angela, you make calls to our key volunteers. Rachel, look at the data and see what maneuvering we can do to reach our vote goal. Tim, call up some of those rich model friends of yours and see what money they have to donate." Everyone resumed their tasks, and the business made the empty office feel partially alive again. She knew that silence was their death knell. A quiet campaign office was just an office. No campaign. She preferred the noise, the wrangling between Angela and Tim, and any other disturbance that reminded her that she was alive at work.

"Sam just called me on my cell. He's about to call you," shouted Rachel from her office.

"Just Sam?"

"Well, both Sam and Parker on conference," replied Rachel.

"Hi, y'all."

"Lily!" they exclaimed in unison. Two states thousands of miles apart could not separate those two.

"So what's going on?"

Parker took the lead. "Florida is unbelievable. It makes the Georgia campaign look like famine relief. We've got cubicles in the office. A staff of 300 and $100 supermarket gift cards to hand out to team leaders to pay for water and food. AND, you won't believe this, but each staff member has only 2 square miles to cover. Not an entire section of the state."

She could believe it.

"Fuck Denver to Mars," shouted Rachel.

"Ohio is the same," Sam chimed in. "I was approved two thousand dollars to hire a vote corps of paid canvassers. We're paying people to knock on doors. Can you believe it! Don't need volunteers. Actually, people don't want to volunteer all that much here. They're sort of tired of being the center of attention every election year."

"Yeah, same here," said Parker. "People here are so used to cameras and canvassers and callers that they've got entire fake stories about themselves. Fake names, addresses, phone numbers. All designed to avoid the attention. Although my Jewish friends from Connecticut have schlepped down here to persuade their grandparents to vote for Cady, which has caught some of them, particularly Broward County, off guard. But then again, those guys are easily derailed."

Rachel buried her head on the desk. "I hate Florida. Beaches scare me."

"We're inundated with ads every hour on every channel. Including public access. Who pays to have ads on public access?" Sam asked. "Well, I've got to get back to interviewing canvassers."

"Yeah, I got to run too," said Parker. "We miss you guys. We miss Georgia."

"We miss you guys too," said Lily on behalf of both herself and Rachel, whose small freckled face contorted into a new shape of anger. "Good luck."

"That is fucking bullshit!" Rachel exclaimed. "We need to fucking call Denver and tell them we're taking this info to the media. This garbage about 'we're the ones we've been waiting for.' Bullshit. They are if they're paid to." It was at that moment that Lily realized the only reason she was left in charge was to soothe the rancor in the office. To add equanimity. She was someone who wouldn't test Denver's nerves. It had nothing to do with anything else. Least of all her ability to win Georgia.

"Rachel, let me call Denver to see what we can get. Remember, we have all those volunteers. The most in any state." Lily almost convinced herself that the volunteers alone could get the job done. In any event, Rachel appeared calmer. The office resumed its low hum of business, and Lily began compiling her lists of "Asks" for Denver. Ask for money. Ask for paper. Ask whether they really expected them to win this state.

CHAPTER 24

Day two with Lily in charge began smoothly. She took a shower and washed her hair with the vegan shampoo from Gabe's care package. Angela and Tim had reached a truce over the stickers. Angela had discovered that Tim's models could get ten times the registrations that any ordinary volunteer could, so she relinquished the stickers in exchange for management rights. Rachel stated her expletives in her inside voice. The steadfast energy calmed Lily's nerves. It had been a while since she tasted pumpkin spice in a coffee drink, so she sipped her latte slowly, while she reviewed the budget spreadsheet. The clump of zeros looked like a typo. At Heels and Ellsworth, she had followed the transfer of money from one bank to the next. Now, she needed to create money from thin air. They had a large corps of volunteers, and thankfully, some rich ones.

"I'm looking for Lily. Is she back there?" It was as if Denise was reading her mind. She could hear the click of heels and that authoritative voice down the hall.

"Yes, she is. And who might you be to grace us with your presence on this joyful day?" responded Tim.

"Lily?" Denise called again.

"Back here." She prepped herself first to disclose that there were no new supplies for the Ludlow office, and second to ask Denise whether she could donate money for the Atlanta headquarters. The ability to be forthright, and yet beg, must be what separated successful politicians from the rest of the wilted pack.

"Denise, what can I do for you?" She gave her a breezy hug, careful not to squeeze too tightly, offered a cup of coffee, and dusted off the chair. She was a politician already.

"Lily, we have a problem." Denise was more agitated than usual. Her Chanel bag lay unzipped on the floor.

"I don't know how to say this, but some people are thinking of leaving."

"Leave? Are they getting tired? Too much work?"

"No, they were offered paid jobs. On the campaign. But elsewhere. Florida. Ohio."

"Paid jobs?"

"Paid to do exactly what we are doing here for free. Plus transportation and housing. Supporter housing. Who's that guy? Your old boss? Fred?"

"Ford."

"Yes, well he's been calling everyone offering them jobs. We're confused. I'm confused," Denise admitted. Lily was confused too. "We want to stay here in Georgia and win this state. But we also want Cady to win. Do we go where help is needed? Kent is retired and Sarah is unemployed. They could use the money. What should we do?"

Didn't Ohio and Florida have enough unemployed people to fill the canvass ranks? Ford must be calling the Georgia volunteer lists from his sofa suite at the W in Cleveland. Did Denver approve this without telling her?

"Denise, just tell everyone to stay where they are. No need to leave. In fact they are needed here more than anywhere else. I'll find out what's going on." Denise looked relieved. "I also need to ask you for something."

"I know. I was headed over to Office Mart to buy supplies for your office and ours." Denise grinned. "There are plenty of local people willing to donate money. You probably just need to reach out to them and let them know of the dire situation. No sugarcoating it."

Yes, she needed to reach out to all the volunteers and donors in Georgia to let them know to donate to the field offices, not the campaign. First, she would put the kibosh on Ford before he called through to the rest of the state.

"What the hell is going on?" yelled Angela from down the hall.

"Yes?" Lily said, poking her head into Angela's office, expecting to referee. She was surprised to find Tim nowhere in sight.

"All of my key team leaders have all been offered paid jobs." Damn, Ford moved fast.

"I know."

"You know?" Rachel asked from behind her. She rushed into Angela's office, and swan-dived onto the beanbag in the middle of the room with the current week's target numbers clenched in her hand. "I really want to kill someone."

"Denise, my old team leader, just informed me. Ford called them."

"That tight ass motherfucker. Do you know he lost his virginity to his own former nanny?" said Rachel. She rolled onto her back to gaze up at Lily, waiting for instructions. Even from Ohio, Ford irritated her. He wasn't even in charge of the state operations for Ohio, rather he was a regional field director like she used to be. He gave up the title of state field director when he left Georgia. And Denver never officially told her they were a service state, like Alabama or South Carolina, a state where they would organize volunteers for weekend bus trips to the other battleground states. Until she officially heard otherwise, she would encourage the volunteers to stay here. And if Denver wasn't sending any money directly, then why not ask them to donate locally? They were in limbo without any direction. She would run the operations as if they planned on winning Georgia.

"Angela, call up all the team leaders across the state. Tell them not to go anywhere. Tell them to get the word down to all the volunteers as well. We will do a separate conference call later tonight with an update."

"Got it." Angela rushed off to the phones, speed dialing every one of them, to beat Ford to the punch.

"Rachel, pull together a list of donors from our volunteer database. We're going to need to ask for fundraising help outside of Denver."

"Awesome!" Rachel popped right up at the thought of sabotaging Denver and ran off to her office. Lily heard the crack of a new bottle of whiskey opening. This would keep her focused for days. "And Tim …" Lily's voice trailed off. "Where is he?" she asked Angela.

"He's training the models on the acceptable forms of photo ID," Angela responded without frustration.

"Ok. Let's continue to register as many voters as possible by the deadline." She could keep this ship afloat until Election Day. They just needed to move forward one step at a time. Dole out the remaining inventory. Utilize the volunteers to their fullest capacity. And start raising money outside of Denver.

CHAPTER 25

"We got an inventory request from Denver." Rachel announced first thing in the morning before Lily could sip her latte. It had been two weeks since Ford had unsuccessfully tried to steal their volunteers. Each day blended into the next. She had forgotten her brother's birthday and she owed her parents a phone call. They had called twice already in the last two weeks. If only they could text. Each neighborhood volunteer team was tasked with recruiting more volunteers so that they could register more voters before the deadline. Each night they reported back from the field, and then the four of them stayed up late shifting around the targets and updating the database. Repeating the cycle the next day. Lily spent her days recruiting local donors, meanwhile struggling to get clear instructions from Denver. She hadn't finished an entire latte in two weeks.

"What inventory?" They had 7 printers and 5 reams of paper left.

"They are squeezing us dry," said Rachel.

"What inventory?" Lily asked Alex, Wright's assistant, on the phone. "We don't have anything." This was only the third time she had spoken with him. The first was when he hired her. Second, to wish her good luck in the new position. For the last two weeks she had left voice mails and sent emails and received no response. Now, when she finally reached him it was to pillage the Georgia office.

"We need a full list of all resources in every state. We've got to shift them around."

"Since when have we had any resources?"

"Lily, I'm not trying to be difficult but things are getting tight. Florida and Ohio are tied in internal polling."

"What about Georgia? Remember, it's the new Ohio."

"Lily, we need you to fill out the inventory list. Whatever little you have, we need to know about."

"Alex, I'm telling you right now, I'm going to sign off as Georgia having Zero inventory. If you want our 7 printers and 5 reams of paper, you will have to fly down and get them yourselves." Click.

Rachel grinned with approval. Lily had never hung up on anyone before. "Fucking Denver."

"If Denver is scavenging for printers and papers, they are going to send out a nationwide fundraising ask. We need to hit up our local people again. It's been a few days." With only 45 days left to the election, fundraising requests were going to occur daily. "I want to do it before Denver does."

"Yes. It's going out in a minute," replied Rachel.

She was too late.

Denise called to let her know she not only received Lily's email, but an email containing a video from Wright that specifically targeted donors in Georgia.

"It's unclear where the money will go, but he's appealing to Georgia. Should I just go ahead and donate in response to this? Will this money come back to Georgia?"

"Can you forward that to me?" She was confused. Maybe they were going to use Wright's national appeal to help fundraise directly for Georgia? She still hadn't received clear instructions from Denver, other than "operate as usual." She still wasn't told they had turned into a service state.

The video popped up on the computer. Wright, sitting on a metal chair, stared directly into the camera. His t-shirt untucked; his under-eyes darker than her own.

You need to see some of the offensive attacks we're up against. I just recorded a short video on my laptop about Eaves's negative ads.

'Don't they have the funds to brush his hair and use better lighting?" Lily asked.

In the remaining days, we need to be ready to respond to smears like these — and worse.

"We've had the worst smears right here in Georgia. Did you hear about the one comparing Cady to barbeque?" asked Rachel.

We need to show that our supporters will fight back against the Eaves campaign's lowroad tactics. That's why our goal is to bring 100,000 new donors into this movement before midnight on Friday.
That means in Georgia we need 3,000 new donors to step up this week.

"Maybe we will finally get the replacement toner."

This is your last opportunity to match the donation of a fellow supporter and encourage them to give for the first time.

Lily made a quick decision. "I think it's targeted to Georgia for Georgia." She told Denise to go ahead and donate to the campaign this one time.

One day later, reports showed that 4000 individual Georgia donors donated more than 75,000 dollars. Perhaps she could finally stop begging locals to pay for water.

CHAPTER 26

She wanted that $75,000 and pressed Alex to stay on the phone. She pretended she hadn't hung up on him last time.

"You know Alex, if you could swing a copy machine, I'd be very, very grateful. Do you know that I'm a certified pole dancer?"

"Wrong team," whispered Rachel. "But really?"

She shook her head no.

"I also have a direct contact to Prada for wholesale purchases."

"Really?" whispered Rachel. She nodded. Well, Gabe did.

"Lily, you guys are doing a great job with all the limited resources you have. It's noticed by all of us at headquarters."

"Well, I've noticed how effective you are at your job. You're a man who gets things done."

"Wow. Thanks."

"So do you want to wire that money to an account?"

"Lily, I don't think you're getting any portion of that 75,000."

"But it was raised here. I know people who donated. One of them bakes an amazing sweet potato casserole."

"And we thank you for your loyalty to the campaign."

"I read that Cady raised more money in Georgia than Eaves. And he's raised 100 million dollars. 100 fucking million dollars. Where's our share of that money?"

"Georgia is winnable, Lily."

"Alex, tell me the truth, if we are a service state then let me know. I'll organize the volunteers to travel to North Carolina or Florida. What are we supposed to do?"

"Given the volume of volunteers, more than any other state, you guys can really do this. You can really win. We need to do a national assessment of resources. I'll get back to you." This time *he* hung up on *her*.

"We got another problem." Angela rushed in with Tim beside her. "We've got volunteers up front ready to donate here, but they saw that video from Wright and are unsure what to do." Damn Denver. "What do I tell them?" She could hear the clamor upfront, ordinarily a good sign for a campaign office.

"They need to donate locally," responded Lily. "If they have supplies, see if they will leave them. Let all the field offices know to just accept whatever comes in." Angela and Tim clarified the volunteers' confusion. At least they no longer fought with each other. She really didn't know what to think anymore. She was starting to feel guilty asking the volunteers to donate locally. How could she expect the volunteers to take their effort in Georgia seriously when the campaign wasn't? Alex said to continue their efforts and the field plan. But without any real resources, how could they? Ten supermarket gift cards would be a start.

"There's a nationwide conference call tomorrow. Just got word from Data in Denver. Cady will be on it," Rachel explained. "We need to get the word out to the field and the volunteers. I'll send out the dial-in password."

OK. That was something. A call with Cady would help motivate the volunteers and since they did notify them of the call, at least Georgia was on the map. She walked out into the main area which was now teeming with over forty people, unloading paper, pens, clipboards, and water.

"Hello, everyone." She paused for a second and took a deep breath. "Our office really appreciates your donations. We couldn't operate without them. I want you all to be the first to know that there will be a conference call for all staff and volunteers with Governor Cady himself." The volunteers hollered.

"When?"

"What time?"

"As soon as we have the details we will notify you by email with the dial-in password. Please make sure we have your email address. If not, please give it to Tim." The line formed around Tim. Already, she saw people move more quickly with the excitement. They also all signed up to canvass on Sunday during church. This was the kind of momentum she hoped to see across the state.

"Angela—"

"Yup, I'll start calling the field offices and make sure they all know. Make sure to get as many people on this call as possible." Angela dialed faster than the last time.

This was the boost they all needed.

CHAPTER 27

Wright first welcomed the volunteers to the call.

"Everyone, this call is with the Candidate himself to thank his most loyal campaign volunteers and staff from across the country with the work so far and to push for that final six week stretch to Election Day. Governor, are you on the call? Everyone please hold just a minute until the Governor is on the call. Governor, Are you on?"

"Yes, Davis, I'm on. Thank you everyone for all your tireless efforts. I know we've all been working hard. And I just want to say the work is not done. We've got to continue to work harder. When you grow tired at the end of the day and feel like you simply cannot work one hour longer, remember why we are doing this. A better future for our children, our grandchildren, and every American. To all of you in Virginia, Pennsylvania, Ohio, Florida, North Carolina, Colorado, Missouri, Indiana, Wisconsin, Minnesota, Michigan, and New Hampshire, I want to say thank you, but the work is nowhere near done. Let's stay strong until the finish line. Thank you everyone."

Cady didn't even know they were down here. He mentioned every battleground state but Georgia. He had no clue that four staffers and hundreds of volunteer teams ran 11 field offices and organized canvasses and phone banks every day. No one in Denver did. No one but Alex. And he was just humoring her. Maybe he really wanted that Prada bag.

"Fuck my toe hairs. Fuck my goddamn toe hairs." Rachel threw the data reports on the floor. "Why won't they just tell us one way or another what the fuck to do? Are we in contention or are we not?

Denise had the same question when she called.

"Is Georgia a battleground state or not? I'm happy to keep doing what I'm doing, but there is some unrest in the camp. People want to know if they should travel to North Carolina or Florida to help."

Lily didn't know how to answer that. The campaign had left Georgia, no matter what Alex or Wright said. Not a sliver of the 100 million dollars was slated for Georgia. This skeletal staff was all that remained. And the next day, the volunteers would gather at the State Capitol for a rally with the famed civil rights leader Lamar Lovell and hip hop celebrity Young Queasy, and she had to report the latest on the Campaign's efforts. She crawled underneath her desk with a new bottle of whiskey and cradled her bald eagle lamp.

"Lily, you here?" She heard Tim's voice. If she had to mediate another spat between Angela and Tim, she would do it after she'd finished half the bottle. She took a sip and remained quiet.

"I've got some good news."

"Under here."

"Why are you hiding?" He reached his arm out to help her up. She took it.

"Tomorrow. It's going to be awful."

"It's going to be great." Tim placed today's field report on her desk. "We knocked it out of the park today. We are awesome." She laughed at his bravado. Tonight, his overconfidence came as a relief. At least one of them thought things were right on track.

"I don't know what I'm supposed to say. Do I tell everyone to continue their effort? Do I ask them to travel to the other states? Do I tell them to go home and help their kids with their science projects?"

Tim sat down beside her. "I don't know. People like coming here and making calls. Hanging out with others. Tasting everyone's cookies. It's not a job to them."

"He's right." They both looked up to the sound of a deep, raspy voice from the doorway. "May I come in?"

Tim bolted from his chair. "Yes, sir. Please do. Lily, it's Congressman Lamar Lovell himself."

She instantly felt nervous. She was face to face with the man who had been working on civil rights efforts since 1959 and had yet to give up. He had been beaten by authorities and placed in a dungeon-like work camp, just due to his efforts to ride a bus. He had marched, not only with other famous leaders, but with local maids and farmers. He never quit. Even when the situation for blacks in the south improved, he still continued to fight for what was right for any group whom the law neglected to protect. At times it cost him old friends, friends who later told him he wasn't black enough. Yet, he never gave up. He stuck to his principles. Even when he won his seat for Congress in 1986, he refused a limousine ride to the victory party. Instead, along with local police officers, labor workers, and other ordinary citizens, he marched the two miles to the hotel. She had never been in the presence of true greatness before. He would know what she should do. She hid the whiskey bottle under the desk. "Truly, truly an honor. Please sit down."

Tim dragged a chair from the hallway, brushed off the crumbs, and offered it to Lovell as if it was his only child. Lovell leaned back in the metal chair as if it were made of soft leather. He looked more distinguished in person than on the book cover. He patted his forehead with a handkerchief and folded it neatly back into his breast pocket. The mid-September heat of the office didn't faze him one bit. He appeared unruffled and relaxed in his suit and tie.

"I understand I will be speaking tomorrow at the rally. I'd like to get your thoughts on what the purpose of the rally is and how I can help the campaign," he asked. How did she begin? Should she tell him there really wasn't a campaign here? No money? No hope for a copy machine?

"I think your being there will be motivation enough. We have less than six weeks left." She glanced at Tim, who nodded. "But I guess there is something I should tell you." This time Tim shook his head.

"What is that, dear?"

"There really isn't much of a campaign left. We're not getting anything from headquarters. No money. Essentially they've given up on Georgia."

Lovell laughed in response. "Oh, dear. I know that. The reason they have anyone left here is for political reasons. To satisfy me, and others like me. They don't think we can actually win this state. They may have had at one time. But not anymore."

"Sir, do you think we can win?" Tim asked.

"I don't know. Probably not this time."

Tim buried his head in the hood of his sweatshirt. Lily let her pen fall to the ground. All she needed was one person, just one person, to believe that they could win. Her eyes began to water. If Lovell didn't think they could win, then what was the point?

"What do you think we should do?" asked Lily.

"Ms. DeMarco, is that correct?" She nodded. "Ms. DeMarco. It doesn't matter whether the campaign thinks it can win. Or even if I think so. I'm an old man who has seen a lot of fights in his life. Wins and losses. The struggle that began generations ago will still continue long after this campaign is over. So, the campaign has left Georgia. You can do whatever it is you want. The question is, *do you think we can win*? Do you think it is worth the struggle to continue? Do the people who show up here to volunteer every day think that it's worth it for them to continue?"

She didn't know. She had been skeptical from the start. The "change politics forever" Kool-Aid that had infused all those campaign kids had evaded her. And then she went to Ludlow, where nothing appeared to have changed in fifty years. Yet her motley crew of volunteers exceeded the region's expectations, and just when she thought things could turn around, the campaign had pulled out. They needed a lot more people. A lot more money. The volunteers were paying for every bit of the operation themselves. To expect anything more from them was simply implausible.

"I will leave you alone with your thoughts," smiled Lovell. "This old man needs to get his rest before tomorrow." He turned to walk out of the room.

"Sir, if you don't mind, I have one more question," Lily said. "It's silly, but it's something I wondered about after finishing your memoir."

"Yes, dear."

"Why did you wait until 1982 to get a driver's license? How did you work and travel all those years without a car?"

He grinned. "I've always preferred the bus. Always will." Nothing about this accomplished man seemed old or weary. She could feel the throb of his vigor from underneath his suit. He bowed his head goodbye and left.

Tim opened his laptop. "What we need is some Dr. King to lift us up."

"Dr. King? Was he on SNL last weekend?" She figured he was one of Tim's hip hop friends.

"No silly. Dr. Martin Luther King."

"Oh, right."

"Here's a recording of I Have a Dream on You Tube."

"Of course. Not judged by the color of their skin, but by the content of their character. Let freedom ring. I've heard it many times."

"Yes. People say they have. But have you actually listened to the entire speech?"

She lowered her head. "No."

"Well, let's listen to it." He wiped down the computer screen, popped open a bag of potato chips, grabbed a soda from the mini-fridge, and pulled his chair next to hers. They listened as King's voice rose and fell with poetic cadence comparing the Declaration of Independence to a promissory note. Smart metaphor. And, the "fierce urgency of now" was still relevant.

"Pass me the pretzel bag, please," she asked. Dr. King continued.

You have been the veterans of creative suffering. Continue to work with the faith that unearned suffering is redemptive. Go back to Mississippi, go back to Alabama, go back to South Carolina, go back to Georgia...

"That's it," she said. "Everyone has to stay right here in Georgia." Tim smiled and passed her a second can of soda.

CHAPTER 28

State Capitol rallies were not what they used to be, if they used to be anything. Back during Lovell's time, hundreds of people marched miles to descend upon the state capitol. But who congregated at the state capitol these days? She had to pay for parking and Georgia's part-time legislature wasn't even in session. Police propped themselves up on stools with crime novels and sandwiches. Thankfully, a crowd began to form in the demarcated area, awaiting Young Queasy's performance. She found Tim, Angela, and Rachel busily collecting registrations and passing out the campaign decals they received when they personally donated to Cady's website. If the volunteers were going to fund this operation, some of the staff's paychecks would have to as well.

"Are you Lily DeMarco?" asked a tall, thin, black woman dressed in sleek, tight black pants and snug white collared shirt.

Lily nodded in reply. She squared her shoulders to look taller. Her back ached from the months of slouching.

"I'm with Queasy Productions. I wanted to make sure that you understand the line up for today's show."

"Well, it's a political rally. We want Queasy to encourage everyone to vote."

"Oh, Queasy will do his thing. He's first. Then Laurel and then you."

"That's Lovell, Congressman Lamar Lovell."

"Oh, right." She corrected her notes.

"Well, is it possible for Queasy to go last?" The crowd would wait for Queasy. Not sure if they would wait for her or Lovell.

"He can't. He's got a photo shoot for Funyuns."

"Those fried onions?"

She nodded.

"They still make those, huh?"

She quickly ushered Lily off the raised platform and toward the staging area to wait. Lovell waited alongside her. She peered into the crowd as it thickened with anticipation. Some had painted their faces with Cady's logo. Some wore sunglasses with a spinning eyes of Cady's logo. Others wore Cady jersey shirts. Most flashed rally signs with Cady on one side and Young Queasy on the other. She spotted Denise crowding an officer, forcing him to place his lunch cooler in his lap. James and two of his friends waved "End the War" signs. Miss Louise brushed off the glitter that Queasy's production team had been spraying on the crowd from Mr. Louise's jacket. Kent and Sarah held matching signs: "Dawgs for Cady." Elizabeth pushed her way to the front of the crowd. At the edge of the roped area, Lily spotted Luke laughing with a Cady supporter. People had traveled from all over the state, nearly 800 in attendance, at Rachel's last count.

"How are you feeling today?" Lovell asked.

"Nervous. In other states, Cady, or his wife, or the VP, would attend this kind of rally. Today it's just me."

"Ahem," he cleared his throat.

"And you and Queasy. Of course." She smiled. "But, you don't understand. I'm horrible at speeches. I've flopped every one so far. That "crazy, ready for Cady" is a loser."

"Don't say that."

"Not planning on it."

"Dear, of course Cady would be the ultimate attraction for this crowd. But these people know Cady isn't coming. They still came, didn't they? They come every day to volunteer for him right?"

"Why do they keep doing that? Why would they still want to?"

"Because they believe he can win. And they believe they can play a role in his winning. And, don't forget the energy that people experience when they come to the campaign office that just can't be replicated by watching it on TV. Don't they hoot and holler while making those phone calls?"

She nodded.

"Don't they tussle over who can get the most registrations that day?"

She nodded again. Clearly they didn't hear Rachel damn Denver to hell. See Tim attempt to woo the models. Angela scream at his insolence. And Lily hide underneath her desk.

"Something is beckoning them to volunteer. Even though Cady isn't in the office himself. They are united by the marrow of change. Every minute they spend working to get Cady elected, they become part of something larger then themselves."

"I need to keep remembering that."

Young Queasy took the stage and the reverberations of the music slowly drowned out the noise of the rally. The crowd, with arms raised, moved up and down in unison to the beat. It swelled with energy and burst through the roped-off area. For the first time, the cops stood alert. Queasy could've been Cady himself. At the end of the set, Queasy encouraged everyone to vote and to Lily's relief, to stay and listen to Lovell and her.

Lovell took the stage next, and the crowd immediately grew silent in reverence. Most listened carefully to his words. He spoke of the struggles he and others had endured in Mississippi, Alabama, and Georgia to ensure that blacks were not excluded from voting. He spoke of the march to Selma, where he received the scar on his face. He encouraged everyone to vote so that the rights people fought for were not forsaken. Lily surveyed the captive crowd and the surprised looks on some of their faces suggested that many of them were hearing these stories for the first time. He then graciously introduced her as a representative of the Cady campaign and she walked up to the podium. Her hands trembled as she took the microphone. The crowd gazed at her anxiously, awaiting an update from the campaign. Eight hundred faces asked, "What's next?"

She glanced over at Lovell, who was standing on the side of the stage. He smiled in encouragement. She wanted everyone to work hard for Georgia. She wanted to win the state. She knew they did, too. What could she say to persuade them? What could she say to make them believe they could win? She took a breath. Only the truth. She clenched the base of the microphone.

"Everyone, I want you to know that, officially, the campaign has left Georgia. Only four paid staffers remain. We alone are working out of the Atlanta headquarters."

The crowd grew silent for a moment and then began to murmur.

"The Campaign has not asked you all to travel to another state. In fact, they believe, as do I, that the volunteer teams you have created will be enough to win. Georgia has the most volunteers of any state. And we have accomplished more than any other battleground state. States that have plenty of money and staff. We have led the states in voter registrations, and if we continue with our efforts for the next two weeks we will achieve our registration goal."

The crowd began to clap.

"But, I need to tell you something very important." She paused. The crowd stood silent.

"There is no cavalry coming. Not from Denver or New York or Washington D.C., or anywhere else." She felt the weight of guilt being lifted. She wanted to be honest. "We are on our own."

The crowd nodded in understanding.

She hesitated, knowing she was about to disregard her law degree and could potentially be disbarred. But she was no longer the same person who obliged every Partner at the law firm and then willingly signed her own severance agreement without protest. Sometimes following the rules led you down a blind alley. "To continue our effort, we need to contribute all of our money and efforts to the local field offices. Brainstorm about creative ways to fundraise. Sell knock off t-shirts, posters, and whatever else you can to raise money."

The crowd started to cheer.

"Make no mistake. This will be a tough fight. We have to accomplish something that no campaign has ever accomplished in this state and that no state has ever accomplished during a Presidential campaign. But I believe we can win. And when we do, not only will we show the Campaign that we can do more in Georgia than in any other battleground state, but that *we* were the ones who did it. Can we do this?"

The crowd erupted in cheer and answered her, "Yes We Can."

CHAPTER 29

Tim tossed the latest field report on to Lily's desk. "If we keep this up we are going to surpass our registration goal."

Lily looked at the calendar nervously. "I hope you're right." Only one week left until the registration deadline. And then early voting would begin. Things were moving faster than she could keep up with. Every day reports from the field showed increased volunteer activity. She spent the last two weeks groveling for money from every possible donor in Atlanta. As she secured each dollar, supplies were bought, and then quickly distributed by Angela and Tim in long road trips throughout the state.

"You look exhausted," Lily said.

"So do you."

Every night after the field offices shut down Rachel analyzed the data for the day. She moved around the canvass and phone targets based on what was reported from the field. Every "Not Home", "Moved", "Wrong Number", and "Refused to Answer" was accounted for. The target universes shifted each night depending on the number of people left to be contacted in the region, so when the local field teams woke up the next morning they could distribute updated canvass and call sheets. They were a 24-hour campaign operation financed dollar by dollar.

The volunteers' creative fundraising efforts also kept the engines running. Miss Louise cracked open the old printing press, and was not only selling t-shirts, buttons, and bumper stickers, but also curtains and sun shields for car windows, all with Cady's logo. There were Cady cupcakes (a chocolate ganache with marshmallow frosting) and a specialty roasted Cady coffee (a blend of East African and Guatemalan) for sale at the corner bakery. Even dog biscuits in the shape of Cady's smile were sold at a markup. All proceeds contributed to the local field offices.

Rachel taught an online webinar for those volunteers who had access to high speed internet and trained them on the computer data program for their region. For those on dial-up, Angela organized a volunteer courier service, which delivered canvass and call target sheets from the Atlanta headquarters to every corner of the state on a daily basis. Kent and Sarah, who only used a computer to email their son, now boasted about how they worked on the "cutting edge" of technology. Denise negotiated a discount rate with a statewide internet provider and then paid for the installation in a few of the offices. Luke worked as the field offices' handyman to fix broken toilets and windows, of which there were a lot, given that the toilets were old and the anti-Cady sentiment was high. Every other day a rock went through a field office window. People held local rallies at restaurants, barbershops, and abandoned town squares to register the last remaining voters before the deadline. Lily reviewed the field reports several times a day fueled by a sugar-high from Cady cupcakes. The entire state was fueled by sugar and coffee.

"That motherfucker is on the phone," Rachel yelled from her office.

Lily quickly picked up the call. There wasn't anything Alex could say to her. They could reassign all of them out of the state, but it didn't matter. None of them would go.

"What's up?"

"Lily, you guys have done an amazing job. You're on your way to exceeding your registration goal." She needed to cut-off Wright's access to the battleground states' status updates. "There are going to be countless opportunities for you and the remaining staff in Washington."

"Alex, why are you calling?" She sensed the hesitation in his voice.

"Georgia is officially going dark. We are taking the offices off our website and it's not slated for any more media buys. You can still remain there."

"That's all? We're on our own? We've been on our own since the beginning." And she hung up. She felt relieved that she no longer had to deal with Denver. She knew she wasn't going to get any help. But at least now there would be no more interference.

"Parker just called on my line. Said your line was busy." Angela hovered.

"Yes, I was on the phone with Alex in Denver. Here's the newsflash: Georgia is on its own."

"Like we didn't know that already."

"That's what I said. What did Parker have to say? How's Florida?"

Angela looked nervous. "She didn't seem to know for sure, but she was asked to find housing for a busloads of volunteers by this weekend."

"Housing? That means they are coming from out of state."

"Right. And there are only two states close enough to Florida. South Carolina or Georgia."

And the battle continued, Lily thought. But this time she would be ready.

"Rachel?" she called out. "We need to send an email to the Georgia listserv."

"Those motherfuckers!" Rachel yelled from her office. "They've cut our communication access."

"What the fuck?" said Lily. They were squeezing the last bit of water out of a cactus.

"Don't worry. Just give me two minutes. I can hack into it."

"You sure?" she asked.

"Yes, definitely. I can do it."

Lily resumed drafting her email to the Georgia listserv. She wanted to reassure everyone that they should remain here.

"OK. I'm in. Send me your email," said Rachel.

There had been a flutter of emails sent over the last few days. What could she title it to make sure people actually opened it?

"Fuckballs! Wright just sent it out," Rachel screamed from her desk.

"What does it say?"

"*Go Where the Fight is: Go to Florida.*" Shit.

"I've got ours ready. Let's send it out right on top of theirs." Rachel scrambled to load the server with the drafted email, while Lily applauded herself at the timing of it. She titled it *Georgia: The fight is here.*

CHAPTER 30

Everyone had been right. They surpassed the registration goal of 175,000. They registered over 200,000 African-Americans and other minorities as well, adults between the ages of 18-35. They officially changed the voting landscape in the state. Lily wished she could throw a celebratory party, but now they had less than three weeks to figure out how to get all those newly registered people to vote. She and Rachel pored over the data and maps, exhausted. Rachel was on her fifth cigarette and second whiskey and it was not even noon. Lily drank more now than she ever had in New York. She grabbed a beer from the mini fridge, which at this point was stocked with only beer and energy drinks. She stumbled into the volunteer area and grabbed a day-old doughnut for lunch. She scraped off the colored sprinkles and began to lick the chocolate frosting. The sugary coating mixed with the beer gave her the shot of energy she needed for the next few hours as they prepared for their final statewide training for GOTV, "Get out the vote."

"I've assigned the precincts that need to be covered to each field office," said Rachel. "Every team has a lot, I mean a lot, of people to cover. They're going to need to canvass and call around the clock. Even with the early vote window."

Lily looked at the data. She still couldn't assess it as quickly as Rachel, but she trusted whatever Rachel said. The early voting period — 45 days before the Election Day — had already begun. And the Eaves voters were outvoting them.

"It's a big event in those little towns. They dress in their Sunday best, cast their ballots, and have lunch at the local diner," Angela pointed out. She peered at the same data as Lily. "Maybe we should have exclusive interviews with America's Top Talent and The Single Pad at the poll locations."

"Well, that's what the GOTV training is for. To teach our teams how to make sure people go vote." It was the last workshop they would offer. After that, the volunteers across the state would be responsible for getting everyone out to vote. The GOTV training was all that was left.

"Let's go." Tim exclaimed as he struggled to carry three boxes overflowing with documents. She thanked Wright for leaving at least one guy on staff. "I got a call from the union guys. People are there already." Luckily, the last union left in Georgia still had a meeting hall.

"Are you guys ready?" Lily was delighted that Angela and Rachel were in charge of today's training. Audience questions made her brain swirl more than her moot court judges had in law school.

"Got it all covered," said Rachel.

"We're going to rock this," replied Angela.

The four of them, along with the members of the statewide volunteer teams, assembled in the union's meeting hall. The mood was cheerful, but also serious. Everyone understood that it would take an enormous effort actually to get the new voters to make it to the polls. Many had no idea where their voting locations were. Others still needed to secure a photo ID. Rachel glided up to the stage, with her data spreadsheets projected onto a screen. She provided a point by point analysis of every precinct with each precinct's voting turnout model needed to win. The volunteers listened attentively. Winning was an actual concrete number and it didn't involve changing the minds of Eaves's supporters. There were enough votes out there for Cady to win. She saw how hopeful the volunteers looked when they heard these numbers. Sure, they were daunting, but they had a goal. People often need a goal, she thought. Just to keep going. Right now her goal was to keep everyone else going.

"I'm passing out the precinct assignments to each group. As you'll see, I've listed the name of the actual precinct as identified by the local elections board, and the number we've assigned them according to priority. Precinct 1 for each group is highest priority, which means the greatest number of votes is in Precinct 1. They are listed in descending order."

The volunteers reviewed their precinct lists. Those teams in the urban areas had 5 precincts to cover with thousands of votes from each precinct. The rural areas had 10 precincts that stretched from one end of the county to the other.

"We understand there are lots of precincts and people to cover, which is why we've prioritized them for you. If you have enough volunteers to cover Precinct 1, then move on to Precinct 2. But you need to be able to cover the precinct fully. Remember, early voting will continue for the next 30 days. During early voting, people vote at their county board of elections. The more people we can get to vote early, the fewer people we need to worry about on Election Day. During this period you need to increase your call and canvass shifts. We will get nightly reports from the Secretary of State's office as to who has voted during early voting. We will then match this data to our data, and as people vote, we will remove them off your call and canvass list. The numbers you have on your list will hopefully go down by Election Day, if people vote early. On Election Day you will need to monitor the precincts for turnout. Angela will explain how you do this."

Angela lunged to the podium. "Yes, it is so easy. You guys will kill it!"

The volunteers remained skeptical. Lily was glad she was on the sidelines for this one.

"Each team should elect a team captain. Everyone take a minute to do this." The volunteers shuffled a bit, but overall remained quiet. No one leaped at the opportunity to lead. Except for Denise. She was quickly appointed Captain for the Ludlow crew. She flashed Lily a thumbs-up.

"Really, it's not a big deal. We just need one person in charge who will report to us from the field."

Slowly people rose from their seats and offered their assistance. Angela sighed with relief into the microphone.

"Now, like I said, the team captain will report, in a wiki document, the number of people who have voted from each precinct at 10 a.m., 2 p.m., 4 p.m., and at close, 8 p.m.," Angela continued.

"How will we get the numbers?" someone shouted. Others muttered in echo.

"That's exactly what I'm going to tell you next. You will have a poll runner who will run to each precinct and ask for the numbers from the elections office. There is a representative from both political parties at each precinct."

"So that means we need to assign a poll runner?" A newly minted Team Captain asked.

"You got it." And the teams resumed with assignments.

"Now you also need people to sign up for call shifts and canvass shifts. Call shifts began early, 7 a.m. when the polls open."

"Isn't that too early?" Someone shouted. "Who wants to get called at 7 a.m.?"

"It's Election Day!" Angela retorted. "We're going to call our voters until they go vote. In fact, we're going to start calling tonight and continue to call until they vote. Early Voting has begun. If they get annoyed with you, tell them to go vote and then you'll stop calling."

Volunteers mumbled quietly in response.

"Aren't there robocalls Cady can do? My cousin in Ohio got a call from the President himself reminding him to go vote." One man pointed out.

Angela beckoned Lily to come to the microphone. She had just missed out on not having to say anything.

"Hi, y'all. Yes, sir. You're right. There are plenty of calls that could be made from Cady or even his wife, which would help our effort. But, as I said at the rally, we really are on our own. Which means there will be no robocalls from Cady. In fact, there will be no television ads either. You and everyone here and every volunteer you muster up from now until Election Day will be the ones reminding them to vote, where to vote, to bring that photo ID when they do, and helping them get rides if they need them." And with that Lily returned to her seat. She already felt tired for the volunteers.

Angela returned to the microphone. "Guys, this is doable. Yes, it is hard. But we know we can win this. The numbers are right here. All it takes is a simple phone call or a knock on the door. It doesn't take anything more than that. All that money and media elsewhere, they don't matter. We've got the lists here. We can do this."

The crowd began to nod in agreement. "Yeah. We can do this! " Denise shouted and stood up. People were instantly charmed by her looks and enthusiasm and stood up with her in solidarity, repeating her cry.

Lily nodded to Tim and he flipped on the music. "*Ain't no stopping us now*" began to sound through the speakers. That did the trick. People started swaying to the music. Some popped open sodas and unwrapped baked goods they had brought to share. For the next hour people danced to Tim's playlist. They grew excited to handle the next phase of the challenge. Lily felt guilty because she wasn't excited. Rather, she felt cheated by Wright, Alex, Denver, and, well, Cady himself for abandoning them. And then she felt guilty for feeling cheated. It was a never-ending loop of anger and guilt. Maybe she just needed another donut.

"You ok? You seem tense," Rachel asked Lily.

She laughed in response. For once Lily was tenser than Rachel. She knew she was in bad shape. "I need to know how this will all turn out. I can't wait any longer."

CHAPTER 31

Lily woke at her desk with the ink from the field reports imprinted on the side of her face. Rachel slept on the floor in her sleeping bag, with her laptop and cigarettes within arm's reach. She had essentially moved into Lily's office, as her own was too far away to discuss anything without screaming, and they had to discuss something every second these days. Two weeks into Early Vote, and every night they reviewed the results from the Secretary of State's voting data. Where were people voting? Who was voting? And the more crucial question, who was not? Then they would report down to Augusta, Athens, New Bethel, Savannah, and every region of the state. Call and canvass those who haven't voted. "We've called them," the team leaders would say.

"Call them again."

She wandered into the reception area to make some coffee, sidestepping Angela, who had found a nice encampment right outside of Tim's office. She'd never get too close to him, but she was never too far away, either. Tim's gentle snoring was rhythmic, almost prayer-like, as if his dreams served as a constant plea for victory. The coffee was gone, and Lily found herself walking in daylight for the first time in days. The air had the perfect cool crispness that only fall could bring. It was always her favorite season. In New York, she would wake up early to run in Central Park around the Reservoir through the brilliant colors of the leaves. Afterward she would grab a coffee and a croissant at *Le Bakery* and a paper for the commute down to her Midtown law office. Now, fall signaled the impending end to a campaign. A changing of the guard for the country. And she had a small role in this.

Donut Palace was the only place open this early, and she bought coffee and pecan delights to last for an entire day. She glanced at her watch: 7:05 a.m. The polls would be open and they would start the daily cycle again. The repetition was comforting. She knew what to expect now.

"Lily, you've got to see this." Tim rushed outside the doors to help her carry breakfast inside. "I just can't believe it." This time his voice choked a bit. Lily instantly was worried.

Everyone was crowded around the TV screen which was turned to NTN, the 24 hour news station.

The news reporter, wearing a scarf and overcoat even though it was only October, stood in front of a long line of people.

"Reporting live from Fulton County, in Atlanta, Georgia, the line to vote outside the polls reaches nearly half a mile long. It is over a two hour wait. The elections superintendent said he has never seen anything like this."

The network then quickly switched to another reporter. This time a man, but in the same, winter clothing.

"Jane, that is the exact same thing we are seeing over here in Gwinnett County. Long lines of people waiting to vote. It's still two weeks until Election Day, but they want to vote now. We spoke to a gentleman earlier who is 70 years old and this is the first time he's ever voted in his lifetime. The elections office said they have never seen turnout among African American voters like this."

Nearly 80 percent of the people in line were black or young people. Lily noticed Angela's eyes tear up. Tim simply shook his head in disbelief. She couldn't believe it either. Rachel sat in shock.

"Rachel, what precinct are those?" Lily needed factual confirmation. She needed to know that they were the precincts that they were targeting. Rachel opened her laptop and punched in her magic numbers.

"Tier 1 in both Fulton and Gwinnett."

Tim and Angela jumped up and hugged each other for the first time. Lily embraced them and Rachel shouted expletives of joy. They cheered and cried together, dined on donuts and coffee as they began to receive calls from across the state. Team leaders saw the reports as well. Their work was beginning to pay off. For the next three days, long lines appeared across the state. Every day, NTN reported from counties and precincts with long lines. All of which were their Tier 1 precincts.

Then on Thursday, NTN reported at mid-day:

"The lines now are several hours long. People, while jubilant, are beginning to look a little weary. The rules prescribe that if you are in line at the time the polls close you will be able to vote, not matter how long it takes. But if you leave the line, you have to go come back another time to vote."

"Holy shit!" Rachel exclaimed. "We've got to make sure they stay in line."

If people left for any reason, the chance of them returning was slim. "We've got to get water and snacks to those in line," said Lily.

On cue, Angela and Tim began calling the team leads across the state to collect food and water. If the lines persisted, with 10 days left until Election Day, they would need as much as they could get.

"The team lead for Gwinnett is on his way to that precinct. He's even got people who will place-hold for them if they need a bathroom break," Tim reported.

Lily sighed relief. "Great. No matter what, people need to stay in line. Rachel, let's send an email request to the listserv for water bottles and granola bars."

"Got it."

Angela paused for a moment. Her eyes watered again. "It's unbelievable." Lily squeezed her hand and nodded in agreement. They watched as the TV camera panned out along the line. A line mostly of minorities, old and young, looking tired, but hopeful and excited to vote. She had never seen anything like this in her lifetime. Not in America.

"Yes we fucking are!" Rachel yelled at the top of her lungs. "Yes we are!" She shook Lily's shoulders and shouted directly into her face. "Yes we are!" This time Angela joined in with arms clasped around Rachel as the two of them spun each other around until they were out of breath.

"The phone doesn't stop ringing," Tim added. "I got a call from Michigan, and now the lines in Georgia are reported nationally on NTN. The guy said his own volunteers were so inspired they began extra shifts."

Each of them received calls from organizers from the other states as news of the long lines made national television. Parker called from Florida. "You don't need those supermarket gift cards."

Lily laughed. "No, I guess we don't."

The call she didn't expect was from Alex in Wright's office.

"We've seen news reports in Georgia. Fucking amazing." She wanted to not care what he thought, but she did.

"I've called state directors in Ohio and Florida and told them to stop siphoning off resources from Georgia."

"Resources?"

"Well, volunteers."

Lily laughed. "They weren't going anywhere."

"Yeah, we noticed that. We started to siphon from South Carolina and Maryland. Not as good as the Georgia volunteers. Also, Wright greenlighted media buys on the local channels. And, there's one delivery truck of yard signs headed for Florida which is now diverted to Georgia."

"That's all great, Alex. But you know what we really need. Who would send us over the top to the finish line?"

"I know Lily, but Georgia is simply not on his schedule."

She returned to watch NTN. News coverage of the long lines was interrupted by the announcement of Cady's campaign schedule for the last week of the election. Included were last-minute campaign stops in Florida, North Carolina, ... and Virginia.

Election Day

Ramal Cady is the first African American elected as President of the United States. In addition to Florida and Ohio, he won the southern states of Virginia and North Carolina. He did not win Georgia, but he won a 47% share of the total votes cast and more total number of votes than any previous Democratic Presidential Candidate in the state.

CHAPTER 32

Lily changed into heels in the bathroom of the D.C. Armory. It was the first time she had worn anything other than sneakers since arriving in Ludlow nine months ago. Gabe bought her the latest Prada peep toes from the fall line as a victory present to wear to Cady's staff ball. They matched her red gown perfectly. Ford and Gianna made a beeline for the bar to buy lemon drop shots, and Tim and Angela scampered to secure a table. Nearly 3,000 staffers and key volunteers poured into the ballroom quickly after waiting an hour in the long, cold security line. They scrambled to find their own corner of the room in which to reunite with their fellow campaigners. Excitement was an understatement. The mood was elevated to another stratosphere. Actors and other famous campaign surrogates passed through the crowd, not allowing any pictures or autographs, but to celebrate alongside the staff and volunteers. Three stages were set up for the evening's events. The center stage awaited Wright, and finally, Cady himself. Cheap beer flowed like water, and blocks of cheese purchased from a wholesale foods store were cut into tiny pieces and served on soggy crackers. Even with Cady as President, Wright still held the purse strings tightly. Lily searched the crowd for Denise and Elizabeth, her allotted "plus twos" for the ball

Gianna passed the shots as Ford shook hands with passers-by. Parker skipped hers. Lily raised an eyebrow in question. "I'm pregnant," she whispered in Lily's ear. "We're getting married in a couple of months." She glanced lovingly at Sam. "He got a job at Commerce and I've got a job in marketing for a non-profit. We're moving here in a month." Sam winked back at her. Gianna forced a smile and cast a forlorn gaze at Ford.

"Wow. A baby and a new job. You really deserve them," she said and gave Parker a hug. They were young, but having seen the two of them weather the campaign, Parker's near-death experience, and then two months of separation, she knew they would be just fine. They experienced more obstacles in nine months than most couples experienced in a lifetime.

Rachel raised her shot glass in toast. "Fuck Denver!" They responded in kind. "Fuck Denver!"Including Ford, despite the fact he had secured a job on the coveted transition team for the White House.

"Ford, it's a good thing you're going into the White House, because now I can harass you every day about making sure The President stays on his toes," Rachel jibed.

He smiled in response. "I'm looking forward to it. Where would we be without the unions and you?" Rachel smiled widely at the prospect of her next position as lead Data Manager for the National Teacher's Union. She had already moved to D.C. two weeks before.

"How about you, Lily? Are you coming to D.C.?" Angela asked.

The group eagerly awaited an answer. Since December she received periodic phone calls from Angela, Tim, and Rachel encouraging her to make the move. She had spent the post-campaign-pre-inauguration months back home in Paterson, with a gym routine that rivaled a sixteen year-old cheerleader, meanwhile watching the entire seven seasons of a punk rock teenager who slew cheerleader vampires on DVD. She wandered aimlessly throughout the mall, as each store front cycled through its holiday sale displays. She moved the furniture out of her apartment and into her parents' basement. Rick packed up his yoga studio, and Rita recycled the magazines to make room for her belongings. She had finally agreed to sell the apartment to Jerry. She had scheduled a visit to Ludlow in February. That was the most she could plan for the present.

"I don't know. I did get a job offer back in Georgia. At the state party."

Ford looked puzzled. "Why? It's a waste of your talents. There's no chance that state will turn Blue any time soon."

"I'll figure it out." She didn't belong in D.C., and returning to a corporate law office in midtown Manhattan seemed as foreign to her as welding bridges.

"I want to go to Justice," Angela announced.

"And so do I," said Tim.

"Justice needs the both of you," Lily replied.

"You know, Lily, we *did* win. We did everything we could in Georgia and that was all we could do," Angela said.

"I know." After the polls had closed, they crowded around the television reviewing the poll-watchers' reports of voter irregularities. They listened as each battleground state reported blue. When NTN reported Georgia too close to call at 9 p.m., she felt she had won the lottery. She chanted "*Crazy, ready for Cady. Crazy, ready for Cady. Crazy, ready for Cady*" louder than any supporter she had heard at a rally, while simultaneously dancing the Roger Rabbit sideways. She sprayed champagne all over Rachel and her data. She ripped the poll watchers' reports into pieces and sprinkled the room with the confetti. She turned up Young Queasy's jam on the music player and dosey-doed with Angela. She threw Tim on the desk, crawled on top of him, and made out. She canceled her tentative plans to move to Canada. She and Rachel ran out into the empty parking lot with Miss Louise's shotgun and the bald eagle lamp. Rachel tossed the lamp high into the air, and Lily aimed and fired. She missed, hitting the brick wall that divided the parking lot from the neighboring building. The eagle lamp crashed into pieces on the ground. The two of them cheered, took a swig out of the whiskey bottle, and ran back inside the office. Then at 9:17, NTN listed Georgia in the Eaves column. By 9:40 she had crawled into bed, avoiding phone calls urging her to celebrate Cady's win at the Atlanta donors' party at the W, and cuddled the champagne bottle. She stayed in bed the next morning watching reruns of The Ex-Housewives of Atlanta. She was temporarily absorbed by Candace, a recent 40 year-old divorcee who just secured her first job as a receptionist for a local recording studio. Eventually, Rachel and Tim forced her out of the apartment and into the office. It was time to break things down. The volunteers had slowly packed up their belongings, emptied two months of trash, and washed the three pyramid piles of coffee cups. She had listened as they retold their celebration stories from the night before, and had watched others laugh and cry as if the reality they woke up to that morning far exceeded the beauty of their dreams.

The Armory grew louder as the alternative rock band "Skeeball High" took stage right. A large crowd swelled closer to the stage as the band began to play its breakout hit. A few even managed to stage dive, and the crowd caught them effortlessly. The music filled the ballroom and people danced, cheered, and imbibed more cold beer, without a single worry on their faces. After one set, the band retired, and moments later the crowd shifted to stage left, as the hip hop star "Nay-K" pulsed through his rhymes. The crowd jumped up and down to the beat. Lily hung back and indicated for the others to go ahead without her. She'd hold down the table.

Elizabeth rushed over to her with a cheap beer in one hand and an envelope in the other. "What a journey, dear. What a journey." She squeezed Lily's hand tightly. Lily missed Elizabeth's French toast. Rita had tried to replicate it, but to no avail. "Have you decided what you're going to do next?"

"No. I'm not sure."

"I do hope you return to Georgia. I know Luke would like to see you, too." He had said the same words to her a few days ago on the phone. "Miss Louise, Kent, Sarah, and James, all send their love."

"I do miss them. Kent and Sarah must be wearing matching Bulldog sweaters by now."

"I almost forgot. This came for you at the office." She handed Lily the envelope.

"Office?"

"We have a potluck dinner once a week at the campaign office. Sometimes we brainstorm about fundraising for broadband internet at the library. It's slated to be cut in next year's budget. But then sometimes we just gab. Catch up on our week."

"Everyone?"

"Yes, and I've finally perfected my fried pickle poppers with pimento cheese."

"Oh, wow." She bit her lip to hold back her tears. "I can't wait to visit."

"I'm going to dance. Want to join?"

"Maybe later," she replied. Elizabeth forged a path through the buoyant crowd.

The envelope, addressed in handwriting to the Ludlow office, had no return address. She pulled out a newspaper clipping from the local Monroe County register. It profiled Lowell Quarterman, the new County Coroner, and the first African American candidate to be elected to this office in the county's history. He looked 15 years younger in the photo, but his smile beamed through the wrinkled, aged newspaper. In the margins, he wrote. *Miss Lily, Yes We Did! L.Q.*

"Yes, we did, Lowell." She took the last sip of her drink and let the tears stream down her face. "Yes, we did." And she joined her friends in the middle of the dance floor.

ACKNOWLEDGEMENTS

Thank you for Stacy S. and JoBeth A. for housing and caring for me. Thanks to my volunteer teams for exceeding my and everyone's expectations. My readers and cultivators-Lance O., Matt W., Rusty D. and the Sackett Street Writers' Workshop. And Kris P., without whom none of this would be possible.

ABOUT THE AUTHOR

Natasha Patel was born in Atlanta, Georgia and lived in San Francisco and New York City before returning to her home state as part of the field staff of the 2008 Obama campaign. Natasha got an early start in politics as an intern for Senator Sam Nunn while attending the University of Georgia. She earned a law degree from the University of California, Hastings and a master's in psychology from Columbia University. She now lives in Atlanta where she's assembled a career made for a renaissance soul. Learn more about the author at http://larensoul.wordpress.com.

Made in the USA
Charleston, SC
22 February 2013